THE HEAD OF THE BULL

To order, contact
CHASE PUBLISHING
A Division of A.C. Chase Associates LLC
P.O. Box 1200, Glen, NH 03838
Tel: 603-383-4166 Fax: 603-383-8162
http://www.chasepublishing.com

THE HEAD OF THE BULL

AND OTHER SHORT STORIES

Philip Edward Duffy

CHASE PUBLISHING

THE HEAD OF THE BULL
AND OTHER SHORT STORIES

Cover illustration reprinted by permission of Heracleion Museum, Archaeological Receipts Fund

Library of Congress Catalog Card Number: 99-74619

ISBN: 0-9629651-3-8

FIRST EDITION

10 9 8 7 6 5 4 3 2 1

This book is a work of fiction.
Any similarity to persons living or dead is purely coincidental.

To order, contact:
CHASE PUBLISHING
A Division of A.C. Chase Associates LLC
P.O. Box 1200, Glen, NH 03838
Tel: 603-383-4166   Fax: 603-383-8162

A part of us always resides in someone else—this book is dedicated to my wife Natalie

CONTENTS

We live imprisoned within our own assumptions, never suspecting the existence of any other world. But now and again, the story of struggles in someone else's world tears us from the darkness of our own enclosure.

Philip Edward Duffy

THE HEAD OF THE BULL

A single man with a house and a good income as a broker was attractive to many women, but Arthur Windsdale had always remained alone. He never found exactly the woman he wanted—at least that's the way he explained it. At work, he was always busy with the investments he handled, and when he had a vacation, he traveled to foreign lands. This year was no exception, and he went off to Ireland—not to Dublin, nor even to Belfast or any of the larger cities. Arthur wanted to see the country, visit the out-of-the way places, and listen to the people who tell the legends in that rich language which rivals the written words of its books of history.

Late one evening, Arthur came to an inn where he was able to mix with local men sitting about in the pub. It took very little prompting from Arthur to make them lower their glasses of stout and tell him stories about the fog-covered bogs that surrounded the place.

"What is the tale that a stranger like me should know about this place?" he asked.

There was a calculated pause, the kind of delay that is fostered by old Irishmen when they want to tantalize a foreign ear.

Then one of them began:

"Do ye know about the great bull that appee'red to one stranger here? The visitor was a man very much like yourself, an American, an' he had his doubts about the story we told 'im until he took a walk alone in the bogs one night. As the light was fading, he suddenly heard the thunder of its hooves, and the fear came upon 'im."

Arthur was pleased; he knew now that the richness of the place would be fully shared with him. He was given another glass of stout so that his mind would soak in the words more effectively. The old man continued:

"I suppose the American visitor to these parts might not have been so frightened if a whole bull had come into his sight. He would have known enough to get away from the place. But the terrible thing was that the bull appee'red only as a huge head, lookin' down upon 'im out of the haze. And it rocked back and forth and lowered its great horns as if to charge, then raised its head again and snorted so that the mist came out of its nostrils. There was fire in 'is eyes, and the stranger knew that nothing good could come of it all. The poor man tried to tell 'imself that the beast was not real, but it wasn't just the sight of 'im that made for the terror—he could smell the bull and hear the snorting sounds and feel the fury. The stranger panicked and ran back here where we sit. We tried to settle 'im down by telling 'im he was safe here in the house, as long as he didn't venture forth too far in the mornin', and certainly not at night."

Arthur was curious to know whether any of these old men really believed the stories that they told, so he asked them outright:

"Do any of you really believe in tales like that?" he asked.

Of course the old men knew they had a sitting duck. What kind of stranger would come to their village to ask about legends unless somewhere deep inside he couldn't quite get them out of his mind. The old men knew how to answer such a question.

They knew the Irish way that doesn't quite answer anything directly. So after the usual delay, it was another man who spoke:

"Wel' now, ye know, we wouldn't want to make ye believe anything that ye don't want to take into yourself. But ye have to remember that we didn't make up the story. It was told to us by that stranger when he came back from the bogs."

The night continued, the stout was raised many times, and the fire burned on the andirons until it was time for sleep. Arthur went up to his room in search of a good night's sleep. Just before climbing into bed, he pushed open one of the small casement windows and looked out into the darkness. There was moonlight playing upon the puffs of clouds that moved along the tree tops. As the wind moved the branches, the moonlight came through and then faded, only to come again. Night sounds came from the hills and bounced off the rocks, only to be muffled by the humus that surrounded the inn.

Arthur went to bed and managed to fall asleep. But rest was hard to come by because his dreams were strong, and he felt himself struggling with an unknown assailant. Suddenly he saw the head of the bull, large and frightening with eyes bulging and nostrils flared. Arthur was in that terrible time when sleep creeps out upon you, then gives way to a waking state that is only partial, only to be subdued into sleep again. It was no longer possible to distinguish what was real from what was dream, and he could no longer find any rest.

In Arthur's dream there was one thing different from the legend he had been told. As the bull appeared and reappeared, it faded away and was replaced by the heads of two women, one almost superimposed on the other. One woman's face was coarse, and her eyes were full of hate. The other face, just behind it, was that of a beautiful dark-haired lass with lovely eyes and a lilting voice that called to him as strongly as any woman ever had. Arthur wanted her and wanted her so much that his hands groped for her as he slept.

At breakfast the next morning, Arthur met the old men again. They were friendly to him as before, but there was a twinkle of mischief in their eyes when they asked him if he had a good night's sleep.

"Fine, fine," said Arthur, afraid that his agitation might prompt them to add him to their legend. He struggled to remain perfectly rational. After all, a bad dream may have been the result of the previous evening when his head was filled with ale and Irish tongues. And it had not helped to crawl into a strange bed in the darkness of that inn surrounded by the bogs. Even now, in the fullness of day, Arthur was not prepared for the thing that happened next!

He was quietly sitting there in broad daylight, eating his fine breakfast, when the door to the kitchen opened. Standing there, big as life, was a beautiful Irish lass, like so many of them are. But the fantastic thing that chilled Arthur's blood was that the woman looked just like one of the two women of his dream— like the one with the beautiful face. It was as if the dream had been stored away in the night and brought forth for him to see in the midst of his breakfast. And there was more than that. As she came to pour his coffee and spoke lightly to him, the voice was the same. And suddenly Arthur was seized by an overwhelming desire. He wanted this woman with a passion stronger than any he had ever experienced before. But there was an ominous way in which she would glide in and out of the room—one minute she was there, and the next she was gone. So Arthur experienced attraction and desire and, at the same time, feared something strange.

Each day, when Arthur was due to continue his travels in Ireland, he delayed for another day. Each day, he saw her again, and at night the dream returned with the powerful bull, the hostile face of a woman, and the beauty that had just entered his life. At meals, Arthur could talk with the charmer who had captivated him so completely. He wanted desperately to invite her to act as his guide in visiting all the hills and castles there-abouts, but something kept him from ever doing that. Un-realistic as he knew it to be, there was a pervasive fear that if he took her with him to the bogs, the head of the bull and the two women's faces might appear. In his mind, legend and reality could never be separated again. It was utterly foolish he knew, but each time he was on the brink of asking her, he would clam up again and just sit and watch her comings and goings.

When the end of Arthur's vacation had come, he reluctantly got into a cab that took him to the train, and from there to the airport and the flight across the ocean. And then he was home, back to stark reality.

But rest would not come so easily. His work at the invest-ment house was just as it had always been, but his nights were fretful, and dreams came again and again. Still, being back in America had placed his feet firmly on the ground again. He told himself that it was all in the past, even though he was still filled with longing and fear.

One night he stopped for dinner in a restaurant not far from his work. He was having his usual food with a few extra glasses of wine when suddenly, there at the door of the restaurant, was a woman. She had long dark hair, a radiant smile, and very black eyes. Arthur was sure that it was she—the beautiful one from Ireland. He tried to repel the idea as fantastic, but the similarity was uncanny. Arthur knew that if he had seen her anywhere in Ireland, he would have walked right up to her. Could a simple country lass, by some remarkable coincidence, have followed him to America? Or was there a purpose in this apparition? Arthur looked at her again, then looked down at his own arms and hands, even felt one hand with the other to make sure he was real. Then he cautiously looked up again. It was she! He was sure of it. Arthur stood up and walked over to the woman and greeted her. She looked at him, half amused and half indignant, and then she walked away.

Despite the rejection, Arthur kept looking. Eventually he walked up to her again, and this time he apologized, explained her similarity to a woman he had known, and talked a little about his life. Her expression softened and there was a twinge of amusement in her lilting voice. If this was his line, she thought, it wasn't very imaginative, but it would do since he was an attractive man, and he had a house, and he was a broker. Margaret was even willing to share a drink with him.

The rest of the story was simple enough. They got to like each other, and they dated often. Love was creeping out to cover them, and finally they were gripped by it. They even made plans for a wedding, and it all went so rapidly that everything seemed unreal. Arthur told her he would take her anywhere in the world for their honeymoon, except that when the possibility of Ireland came up, he demurred. They went to the Bahamas.

Marriage settled in after that, and he returned to the brokerage house, and she to her job in advertising. It all seemed well.

After about six months, however, it became apparent that Margaret had another side. She could, from time to time, be arrogant, demanding, harsh, and tempestuous. The moods would just burst forth. At first Arthur thought it could be worked out. But one day he experienced something new and ominous.

He had just had an argument with Margaret when he looked up to see her in back of the kitchen counter looking fixedly at him. Her expression was belligerent, and suddenly the horror of horrors broke upon his mind. Her face looked just like one of the two women in his dreams, but this time it was like the coarse and hostile woman, the one with the hateful eyes. It mattered very little to Arthur that the association was ridiculous and could have no meaning in the real world. He could reject all that. But the association of his wife with the specter was galling. And the two faces appeared more often when he dreamed about the bull, and it became as intolerable to him as when his wife was in one of her foul moods.

Arthur could no longer deny that his wife had a dual character which appeared in the form of two women's faces, just like the women in his dream. Which one was she really? The tensions in his marriage were unbearable, as Margaret periodically shifted from the beautiful face to the hateful one which exploded with anger.

In a desperate effort to save their marriage, Arthur decided to confront her with the two sides of her personality. Much to his surprise, she was unaware of it, believing that with every altercation, it was he who had said or done something to alienate her. She claimed she was only defending herself, and she saw nothing hateful or excessive in her reactions. That was the real problem. No matter what he said, she remained oblivious to the thorny side, the darker side of herself. It all seemed hopeless to Arthur. He despaired of any improvement, so he spent less and less time with her. They were growing apart.

But one day, in a talkative mood, he decided to tell her all about his trip to Ireland and about the legend and his dreams. As he spoke, he became afraid that she would laugh at him or become angry at the implications. Instead, she suddenly became silent. The tale had reached her and had taken hold of her in a strangely powerful way.

A few weeks later, Margaret happened to be in a museum which had a whole wing devoted to statues and paintings derived from great legends of the world. Suddenly, in one darkened room, she was face to face with the head of a huge bull. It was a creation of ancient Greece, the Minotaur from the island of Crete—that terrible bull which killed all the young men or women placed into its labyrinth. The eyes of the bull were made of rock-crystal, and its muzzle was made of shells. Margaret was fascinated, but the vision of the bull suddenly triggered Arthur's Celtic legend and his description of that snorting bull. It was as if the same monster could exist in two places and follow them around wherever they tried to escape. It all flashed before her eyes—the Greek bull, the Celtic legend, and faces of beautiful and hateful women, all mixed together and moving. She became terrified as the lustrous eyes of the bull were fixed upon her, following her even as she moved about. The eyes made her think that, in some way, the beast was blaming her for some evil within herself. And worse, when she looked past the bull, there was a mirror on the wall of the museum in which she saw her reflection—it was the face of a woman full of hate. Margaret had finally seen her second face! She ran to the main lobby and out into the sunshine.

When Margaret got home, she felt a compulsion to tell Arthur about her experience. He tried to make light of it:

"The sight of that bull just reminded you about my story," he said casually. But, as he said that, he remembered the deep effect his story had generated in her.

Margaret remained silent. Her body was shaking as she thought of the bull and her reflection in the mirror. Suddenly she burst into tears.

Arthur had never seen her so vulnerable, nor so accessible to him, and it made him walk over to her, take her in his arms, and lift her up They gripped each other in a desperate embrace. At this moment, she whispered in his ear:

"I know there must be a terrible side to me," she sobbed.

Arthur pulled his head back to look at her face, fearing the sight of it. But when he looked, he saw her usual beauty, without any hate. Her imploring eyes reached out for him.

They clutched each other tightly as if they had found each other for the first time. And after that, life flowed more easily, and whenever they had free time, they were together. They often traveled, inseparably bound to one another, and they went all over the world and saw many strange sights. But they never went to Crete and they never set foot on Irish soil.

THE WINE MERCHANT

He called himself a wine merchant, but most of his life he was unemployed. Albert Charcot was a very little man, about five feet tall and slight in build, but his voice had a resonance that was deeper than one would have expected. He was born in a small French town in the Cévennes mountains and lived within the bounds of that town all his life. As a young man he met Thérèse, an attractive and efficient nurse, who fell in love with him for reasons incomprehensible to her family. They were married, and from the start, they appeared to be happy.

The Charcots' way of life was simple. She worked at her profession, brought in a reasonable salary, and supported them both whenever he was out of work, which was most of the time. During two years of their early married life, he had been able to work for a winery, and this short-lived success was the basis of his calling himself a wine merchant for the rest of his life. Thérèse, his wife, also called him that as a face-saving device.

It was difficult to know why Albert never held a permanent job. He was intelligent, resourceful, and pleasant, and he was a good conversationalist. He presented himself well to society and to possible employers. But there was a certain inanition about Albert, a lack of drive, a "sans souci" attitude that inevitably transmitted itself to his employers and made them replace him. As a result, he got jobs easily, but could never hold them.

The rest of the Charcots, the extended family, did not accept with grace a man who didn't work. Their cultural background did not allow an understanding of this weakness because they came from a long line of Huguenots, that Protestant group in France which prided itself upon hard work, strict religious rules of behavior, and strong family ties. For generations they had been persecuted in France because of their religious beliefs, and their very survival was based upon resistance and active work habits and industry from every member. Within such a community, there was little room for a person like Albert who worked casually from time to time, but otherwise depended upon his bright and industrious wife. At family gatherings when Albert and Thérèse were not present, there was a repeated evaluation:

"What is Albert up to now, or rather, what is he not up to?" Uncle Charles would ask, with an amused expression. The rejoinders varied:

"I hear that he's given up his job at the winery," Cousin Hélène would answer.

"Oh," Uncle Charles would ask, "how long ago was that?"

"About twenty years ago," Hélène would say, as the group broke into laughter, and Charles would continue:

"Is he thinking of getting another job?"

"Yes," Gaston would say with as serious an expression as possible, "he's been thinking about it."

"How long has he been thinking about it?" Charles would persist.

"Oh, about twenty years," Hélène would answer, as another peal of laughter spread from one to the other.

It was an old pattern, and it changed only in the varieties of Gallic humor that could be focused upon it. Despite all the derision, Albert was never excluded from the family—it was part of that hardy stock that they took care of their own. So Albert was always a full member of the family, but he was a member of low standing. Notwithstanding Albert's status regarding work, one would never have discerned his position from his behavior when he was with them. From within his small frame came that resonant, self-assured voice.

Thérèse, of course, suffered from the family's derision of her husband. She too believed in the family's sense of industry, but she loved her husband with that dogged determination with which she had survived everything else. She admired his kindness, his concern for the children, his willingness to help her, his intelligence, and the courage with which he maintained himself among his family and his peers. She, like the rest of her Huguenot clan, could not be subdued by ridicule since for generations they had withstood the kings of France, their cardinals, and of course, that infamous queen, Catherine de'Medici, who had ordered the St. Bartholomew's Day massacre of the Huguenots.

No one could have understood the Charcot family without knowing their Huguenot roots. As the darkening clouds of World War II gathered, the Charcot family, like other Huguenots and much of Catholic France, grew closer to each other in their daily prayers for peace, without taking the aggressive military preparation that should have been adopted. France had had its time of expansion, its conquering Kings, and its Napoleonic legions which at one time had been the most powerful, the most precise, the best-organized military force in the world. But France had slowly moved into a more civilized state. After the Revolution, and then Napoleon, it became hard for any would-be despot to gather the French people into his fold; they remained fiercely independent and unwilling to devote their lives to any leader of military adventures. It was a wonderful trait, but it was also a dangerous one since in the East their German neighbors thought about nothing but tanks, planes, bombs, and Wehrmacht.

When war came to the Charcot family and to France, they
were not ready. England and America were not ready either, but
England had a channel and America had an ocean which gave
them time to recover while France bore the brunt of the
onslaught. France had concentrated upon defense with its
Maginot line. In Germany, the Siegfried line may not have been
any better, but for almost a decade, Germany had spent most of
its wealth upon new weapons and Panzer divisions. Its national
consciousness was focused upon convincing itself that it was a
superior race which must use force to grasp the land and possessions of its neighbors. It led to the inevitable defeat for France
and for the Charcot family.

But there was a collective knowledge within their family and
the other families throughout the Huguenot Temples that
resistance would never be forsaken. The fires of that resistance
were stoked when Thérèse asked Uncle Charles a question:

"Have you heard about Le Chambon-sur-Lignon?" she
asked.

"Yes," answered Charles, that Huguenot town is taking in
refugees, defying the Germans, but it is a very dangerous thing
to do."

"Of course," answered Thérèse, "but it's the only decent
thing to do. They welcome anyone on the run and take them
into their own homes. They take in members of the resistance,
the Maquis. But they do much more than that—they take in
Communists, Slavs and Russians, and especially Jews. All are
welcomed with open arms."

"I know, I know," said Uncle Charles, "and they feed them
and hide them and take them across the border to Switzerland
when they can. There's a death warrant for anyone who does
that. Whole towns have been massacred for defiance and courage
like that."

The members of the Charcot family did what they could.
Exactly how much any of them would defy the Germans, no one

could predict, but resistance was in their blood. For Huguenots, it was an unwritten rule that when you took part in resistance, you didn't talk much to your neighbors about it. It was a form of protection. The less you knew, the less you would be liable to talk if interrogated by the Gestapo. Still, within a family, it became known who resisted and who did not. Several of the Charcots were involved in resistance one way or another, as their ancient heritage rose to the occasion and refused to accept defeat.

However, the terrible day came, as it was bound to come, when the Germans began to take hostages. The first German roundup of suspects took place in the middle of the night. Several Charcots were torn from their homes in their night clothes, and one of them was Albert, that small man who never amounted to anything. During the next week, no one knew what had happened to the men, women, and youngsters who were taken. Then, one at a time, some of them began to drift back to their houses. But there were bruises on their faces, and they had the gaunt look that comes to people cornered in basements where there is no one to help them. A few came back untouched, and a few days later, other men would be arrested. It was widely recognized that under pressure, under pain, they had talked.

Albert was gone a long time. Thérèse was distraught—she knew that Albert had carried messages to the Maquis and that he had helped forge false identity papers for refugees—all capital crimes. And since it was known that people were being taken away and shot, the family feared that Albert might be one of them. Finally, one of the villagers who was returned to his home said he had been imprisoned in a cell near Albert. The returned villager spoke to Thérèse alone:

"He's alive," he said tersely, "but he has had a hard time."

"What have they done to him?" Thérèse whispered in fear.

The man didn't want to go into details; he became taciturn. What good would it do to describe it all to her. And yet he felt he owed her some information:

"They've been questioning him day and night. I want to tell you something remarkable about that husband of yours. He won't talk. He won't give them the slightest bit of information. He gave them his name, and after that he closed his mouth and wouldn't say a word. I can't hide from you that he's been badly beaten."

Thérèse's breath stopped, and then she sucked in the air with difficulty as her whole body trembled:

"My poor Albert. My poor Albert. He's such a gentle soul, such a kind person. He's not made for war and the horrors that follow it in the civilian population."

The villager looked at her with an expression of compassion mixed with pride:

"Actually," he said, "he was the bravest man amongst us. No matter what they do, he won't talk about anyone else. None of us whose underground activities were known to him have the slightest thing to fear. While all the rest had a breaking point, Albert would not talk. I tell you, he will not say a word about anyone else."

Thérèse sobbed quietly and walked from the room, her head hanging low. She expected the worst. She would never see her love again.

But the events of the next few weeks defied all imagination. There were, to be sure, men who were never heard from again. But one day as Thérèse stood in her little garden keeping busy with the chores, she looked down the dirt road, and there in the distance was a man walking toward the house. At first she assumed it must be a stranger, but gradually she recognized the features and the casual walk. It was Albert!

Thérèse rushed to him and embraced him. His face was swollen and covered with black and blue marks, but he spoke clearly, and they huddled together and made it back to their house. Albert would only say that he was all right, but he would not describe anything that happened to him in the cellars, except to say that he didn't have any idea why he was released; he had not counted on it.

After that, bit by bit, the Charcots began to piece their lives together. And when the armistice came, they celebrated like all the others, and they welcomed their young men, the ones who made it back from the work camps and the concentration camps. Eventually, the invaders, who now knew fear themselves, all went back to their homeland, and life began anew for those who were still alive.

The mayor of the small town offered Albert a clerical position in the records of veterans' affairs, a position that he accepted, and soon reports came back that he was doing a good job.

On Sundays, after the religious service at the Temple, the Charcot family gathered once again for dinner and those afternoon conversations and the reading aloud of letters from friends and relatives. It was almost as if nothing had ever happened. The family bonds were still there. A little of their good humor returned, and once in a while they could tell funny stories. But there was one difference. It was a difference that no stranger would have been aware of, but within the family there was a complete transfiguration.

Albert was always offered the most comfortable chair, and Uncle Charles, who used to sit in it, was at one side. When Albert spoke everyone became silent, and they listened attentively. There was a displacement of space which Albert made no effort to capture, but which opened up around him, as if he had always been the head of the family. They never talked about the war, but it was always there. And in a corner of the room, Thérèse would sit quietly watching her husband and holding her head high.

THE CONFIDENTIAL GESTURE

Rebecca was strong, her posture upright, her movements bold, and her speech decisive. Anita was different; she was so shy that she felt her shyness even when she was alone. She wore this shyness like a black shawl that remained wrapped around her, no matter where she was or what she did. It was precisely the differences in these two women which prompted them to rent a house together. Rebecca's forceful personality could release Anita from the blackness that separated her from other people. And Anita furnished Rebecca's need to be in charge, to manage or improve someone else's life.

Rebecca had a boyfriend named Charles, who, like Anita, needed management, but unlike Anita he was quite outgoing and gregarious. The trio worked out well because Charles enjoyed having two women to relate to, Anita was never alone, and Rebecca reveled in managing the lives of two other people. It was almost a ménage à trois, since Charles was at their house much of the time, maintaining his own apartment for most nights.

The reason for Charles' attraction to Rebecca was that he needed her sparkle, her fiery black eyes and streaming black hair, and her vibrant energy. He was not a weak man, and yet he allowed her controlling ways to manage their daily lives in a way that surprised him:

"I sometimes wonder why I let you lead me around," he would say. But there was a smile on his face, and she knew that there was no resentment. It just suited them both.

At first, Charles saw Anita as an accompaniment, as someone who was always there in the background, pleasant and harmless. He was well aware of the striking difference between Rebecca's dark beauty and the beautiful blond hair and blue eyes of Anita. And he noticed that unlike Rebecca, whose every move conveyed energy and determination, Anita seemed to glide about the house with a light touch and flowing movements. Charles could have been attracted to Anita's blond hair and winsome ways, but she had never done anything that required a response from him—so he allowed himself to belong to Rebecca. Charles was well-suited to his intermediate role between these two women because he was an affable, occasionally charming person, passive enough to follow Rebecca's initiatives, and easygoing enough to draw out Anita without frightening her.

It was a cohesive threesome, a comfortable relationship. Living with two friends on a daily basis was more than Anita had ever had. She was thankful to her loyal friend Rebecca because she knew that it was Rebecca's sparkling personality that stoked the fires of this three-way bond. And it was this bond that was her lifeblood, preventing her from closing herself away in that dark shawl of shyness.

It had been like this for four years and might have flowed on like that forever, except that Rebecca concluded that Anita was not moving on to the next step, was not finding other friends. Somewhere deep in Rebecca was a powerful need to fix things in other people, and she saw what needed improvement in the friend she loved. She wanted Anita to go out with men. She even suggested that Charles take her out once in a while:

"It'll be a thrill for her to go out with you and meet other people at some of the parties you go to. She'll feel safe doing that in your presence."

Charles wasn't too sure about the idea:

"Maybe if you suggest it, it will be all right," answered Charles. "Of course, I have a feeling that I'm in for a very mild evening, to say the least."

"I'll liven it up for you when you get home," chirped Rebecca.

"That's a bargain," agreed Charles. "I'll hold you to it."

Anita and Charles were off. It was a quiet evening, as Charles had anticipated. During the rest of the year, they had other outings of the same kind at the homes of Charles's friends. Anita felt safe with her escort. Before she had gained Charles as an escort, she would panic whenever she entered a room full of people. But now she entered as if she were a married woman, with her hand on Charles' arm, and the results were startling. Other men noticed her more, engaged her in conversation, asked her to dance. The miracle was that Anita went along freely. The presence of her escort freed her to act as if all the other contacts were casual interludes which produced no fear. And in her new role, she was more attractive, more engaging, with her wan smile transformed and her face animated.

When Rebecca heard about it all from Charles, she was delighted:

"I was right, you see," she said to Charles. But he was not so sure:

"I don't like it. We're leading this girl along into unchartered waters. She lets men hug her very close when they dance, and I don't think she even knows what she's doing."

"I think it's terrific," persisted Rebecca. "I think we've done something no psychiatrist could have done. She's coming out of her shell."

Only Charles remained skeptical:

"You haven't seen her circulating around, the way she does.

It's not in her nature to be like that."

"You mean, it wasn't," countered Rebecca. "But now she is apparently set free. That was the whole idea."

Charles kept shaking his head about Anita's new contacts with other men:

"It's an artificial transformation," he would repeat.

One evening Charles came to the two women's apartment and found Anita all dressed up to go out with another man. Charles became strangely agitated, and before Anita's date arrived, he took her aside:

"You ought to be careful and move slowly with all these men you've begun to see," he warned. "You have lived most of your life without men, and you have to realize that some of them can be pretty persistent when they're alone with a woman."

Anita looked surprised and perhaps a little pleased at his animation, and she was honest:

"You're right, I don't know all the things that most girls learn in high school. But I've decided that it's now or never."

Charles began to pace back and forth, later grumbling to Rebecca who absolutely refused to share his concerns:

"She's a grown woman," she declared.

In the following months, time hobbled along in fits and starts. Charles spent more and more time talking with Anita, and she responded gently with her shy smile:

"I appreciate your concern," she would say softly. "You've been wonderful."

They spent more and more time talking about themselves, about Anita's childhood, her shyness, her seclusion, her inability to break out, as if she had not effectively broken out of all that in recent months. He kept thinking of her the way she had been, and she reverted to that role when she was with him.

Throughout all this, Rebecca remained the central figure, the one who nurtured Anita and managed Charles. Rebecca was thriving on her controlling position. Who would have thought that a single instant could break it all up?

It came about when Rebecca was in her study one day while Anita and Charles were in one of their intimate chats, sitting in wicker chairs on the lawn. They were not directly in Rebecca's view, but as she moved from her desk to the file cabinet, there was one angle at which she caught a glimpse of them. Their chairs were close, facing each other, so they could speak in quiet tones. At the very moment that Rebecca glanced out, she saw Anita reaching slowly forward with one hand and placing it softly on Charles's hand which was on the arm of the wicker chair. It was one of those gestures that expressed sentiment better than words. Anita's hand rested on his for a moment, and then she slowly drew the fingers back stroking his skin in an inadvertent caress. The confidential gesture was soft, tantalizing, and intimate. There was a slight embarrassment on their faces, as if they had just made a discovery, or as if they had just done something wrong. Anita's gesture was something that she would have done without hesitation in the presence of other company. She would even have done it in Rebecca's presence, but in this instant, very much alone, it generated a powerful impetus of its own.

Rebecca stopped short, stared, and took a fast breath. Quickly she spoke to herself:

"That was nothing," she said.

It was, indeed, nothing she had ever considered—not little Anita and Charles! Not the two of them acting without her directions. Rebecca was dumbfounded, but recovered in her characteristic style. In a flash, she stuffed her papers back in the file cabinet and walked briskly toward the lawn where she took over as usual:

"Anita, will you get us some tea? I need to talk with Charles."

Anita shuffled off, Charles squirmed in his chair, and Rebecca plunked herself down in a chair.

"Well," she asked, "you two having one of your good talks, are you?"

"Yes," Charles answered, "we're talking about Anita's recent dates."

"You're not still worried about them, are you? I think you ought to forget about that and get on with other things. Anita's got her life in control."

Anita came back with the tea. She let Rebecca serve as usual, but nothing was really as usual. The motions were the same, the chatter was the same, but their positions in the chairs were not. They sat more upright, more formally, as if they were at attention. One might have thought they had just met. Each one was taking stock of the others, each alert to what the others said, or how they said it, or how they looked as they said it.

Charles and Anita felt as if they were involved in some kind of collusion. It was the first time they had really seen each other clearly, and in that sense they had just met. Rebecca had grasped the situation immediately, but for the first time she faced something for which she had no instant solution. She was terrific at telling people what to do, but now she needed to tell two people how to avoid their feelings. Rebecca's business was promotion, not coaxing people to pull back. She was baffled, but it would be only long enough to regroup, to rethink.

Certainly the forces of power were upset; Rebecca had no immediate leverage, while Anita, the one who had always been powerless, was in temporary control without doing anything. She had, with time, gained Charles's attention with her shy smile, her dependence, and her needs, so all she had to do at this moment was to remain as she was.

It wasn't, even now, as if Charles and Anita had plotted to create this situation—it had just happened. They felt guilty about something they did not do, something that came upon them, something that was really only a new realization of themselves. It was Charles who raised the issue the next time he sat alone in the car with Anita after returning from an errand. They paused without getting out of the car for a moment, and he put it bluntly:

"Are we feeling something new?" he asked.

She saw his meaning and admitted a part of it:

"We're not quite the same as we were," she said.

"Maybe that's all it is," Charles ventured. "We've seen our-selves in a new light. Rebecca's been a strong force in my life and in yours; there's no denying that."

"She has," whispered Anita.

They sat perplexed for a moment longer. Inside the house, Rebecca counted the minutes till their return without being quite sure what to do. All of them knew that there had been no villain in this threesome. But now, at every turn, that confidential gesture seemed to scream out for wrenching decisions!

In the end, the sense of crisis made them all react in their own natural way, in the only way they could. Anita pulled back, Charles waited, and Rebecca burst forth with energy and action. She was never without resources long. She quickly enfolded Charles, scooped him up, and occupied all his time whenever he came to the house. Charles was now attracted to both women, but he was so accustomed to returning Rebecca's more positive advances that he generally stood by his old position. At times he wavered when he was alone with Anita, and then she responded as strongly as she could with small efforts to reach for her own life:

"Those other men I've been going out with lately," she would say to Charles, "mean nothing to me. They are only a way of trying to be like everyone else, trying to fit into the future that you have tried to help me attain. You've become my guiding light."

"I know you deserve better than to stay at home by yourself," Charles would answer.

He continued to play the supportive role, as she waited for more.

Events moved on faster after that, mostly because Rebecca was moving on as always. She and Charles began having talks about their lives, and one thing led to another until one of them proposed marriage. Rebecca accepted her own proposal and told Anita about it at dinner time:

"Charles finally popped the question to me," she said airily. Charles smiled congenially and nodded his head. They both looked at Anita.

She turned her head gamely toward one, and then the other, and congratulated them:

"What wonderful news," she said, with a full smile. Her cheeks were pale, her lips tight, her body rigid, but her words were all that one might expect. She asked about the expected date, she asked about the wedding site, she spoke about the elaborate ceremony that would be planned, and the honeymoon. She put her fork down, and she talked and talked, but ate nothing.

The day of the wedding came, and it was everything that Rebecca planned—a great church wedding, a great attendance, and a long trailing gown.

The elaborate wedding reception was held in the Talmadge Hotel, the most prestigious place in town, and there was a wonderful band and lots of exciting announcements. When the time came to throw the bouquet to the bridesmaids, Rebecca made sure it was Anita who caught it.

Events had gone smoothly as expected, held together throughout by a loyal groom, a dedicated bride, and their friend of many years. During the wedding party there was much dancing and singing, and there were stories to tell. Nothing was missing, nothing went astray.

But there was a fraction of a second in which something happened, something that would be remembered by the three friends, each in his or her own way. It came about when the groom was separated from the bride for a few moments, as he joked near the bar with his friends from the office. In the midst of all the frivolity, Anita, on her way to the main ballroom, inadvertently walked very close to Charles. So they suddenly faced each other, and he instinctively led her to one side where they sat at a small table, as if for a last brief confidentiality.

Rebecca was in the hall, laughing with friends and relatives, but moving about to be sure to talk with everyone. As she came by the door to the bar, she saw Charles and Anita sitting at the table, but she thought very little about it because she was comfortable and secure—now that Charles was legally her husband. Nonetheless, there was that brief moment when, for the second time, she saw Anita's hand come forward slowly, hesitatingly, in that shy way of hers. It came to rest caressingly on Charles's hand, in that intimate mode, that familiar expression, that confidential gesture. Then she slid her hand back slowly, as if embarrassed that she had gone too far. He looked very seriously into her face, almost expectantly. But soon they both gave a formal smile, stood up, and went their separate ways.

Forever after that, the gesture lived in their memories. Charles and Rebecca bought a new house, and Anita rented an apartment and dated other men occasionally. The close-knit trio was all finished, except that each one remembered the gesture of that gentle hand that rested ever so lightly upon his. And each of them could never forget whatever it had meant, or whatever it meant now.

THE TORMENT AT MONT SAINT MICHEL

The monstrous shadows of the French abbey of Mont Saint Michel and the great stone walls that surround it had engulfed the American visitor, and after that the great structure would never fully release him. James Wilcox was overwhelmed by its great medieval austerity, its awesome history, and its sacred atmosphere, as well as by the sinful and profane events that it had harbored.

But all this came only later. When James Wilcox was a boy, things were simple enough, and nothing in his boyhood would have foretold the troubles to come. After college and later graduation from a school of architecture, he had formed a partnership with another young architect named Ed Hearly. All went well at first, but gradually, relentlessly, a hidden aspect of James Wilcox began to emerge. It all centered upon his ambition which welled up uncontrolled from somewhere deep within himself. James was becoming a driven man. He could never put his ambition out of his mind for a moment, even to rest or sleep. The explosive moment was coming closer when James Wilcox would come face to face with the ominous shadows of Mont Saint Michel!

Day in, day out, James barely contained the burning desire that made him want to produce an original architectural wonder that would flash across the images of the world to dazzle everyone who saw it. But there was one persistent threat in all this—James Wilcox had never clearly visualized what this definitive work would be. He had studied the great architects, especially Frank Lloyd Wright and Walter Gropius, as well as the ancients. But he dared to want something even greater than that, something which would let him stand above all the others. He convinced himself that he could do it some day, but, so far, he had to reject every idea that came to mind. So, there was no respite in his life, and he disrupted every other activity in the office. The constant agitation caused his friend Ed to try to reduce the mounting tension:

"It's O.K. to be ambitious," he told James, "but you have to learn to let up a little once in a while. Be satisfied with a fine-quality building."

Restraint like that was anathema to James, and he was secretly enraged by his partner's remark, so he restated his ultimate goal in sharp tones:

"I never look at it that way, and my life is not meant for rest. I will produce the ultimate work that no one can match. It will be a symbol of everything that I stand for, everything that is my life."

"That would be all right," countered Ed, "but didn't you tell me that you have never been able to conjure up anything remotely like that, even in your mind?"

Jim grew silent and he bit his lip.

During the next ten years, Jim worked on eight major projects. There were four private houses, one office building, a bridge, a memorial tower, and some conference center structures. Each time he finished a project, the reviews of his work were good, but superlatives were always lacking. Each time Jim knew he was no closer to his ultimate goal, and his anger turned upon himself.

Then came the fateful day when Wilcox first saw that great wonder of ancient architecture called Mont Saint Michel. It all began when he made a business trip to France where he was taken to Normandy by his host. They drove along the coast, and soon they could see the water of the channel. Then, suddenly, the ancient structure appeared in the distance in all its majesty! The great buildings stood together on a mound of earth and rock surrounded by the ocean, with only a narrow causeway from the mainland. The central abbey church had a spire about two-hundred and forty feet above the surrounding sea. And there was the monastery and the great fortified ramparts and towers, all rising high above the huddled stone houses near the base of the great mass. It was the most magnificent thing Wilcox had ever seen! He was overwhelmed—struck dumb! There it was, every-thing that he had ever dreamed of inventing himself. For an instant, he thought that he had been so preempted that there was no hope that he could produce anything so great. But as he stared at that marvelous mass of buildings isolated on that mound of earth and rock surrounded by the sea, Jim could see that part of the genius of the place had been invented by nature, not by man. It was as if the hand of God had placed it there in all its glory. James Wilcox was seized by the belief that a key had just been placed in his hand—a key with which he could unlock the secret to his great ambition and relieve his tortured mind. The way to create a work of genius, he decided, was to seek out some natural wonder of the earth and build something that would adorn it still further. The great discovery, the genius, was in the recognition that no human could produce anything this grand alone. Finally, Jim Wilcox believed he was at the end of his obsessive search. He could now turn all his energy toward the creation of his glorious legacy to the world.

Jim pressed his French host into visiting the Mount again and again. The whole experience became a delicious, almost sensual adventure. But he needed one thing more—he needed someone who knew everything about the long history of Mont Saint Michel—someone who could tell him everything there was to know about its past. After much searching, he located a French historian named Jean Camus who was so specialized in Mont Saint Michel that he insisted on living near the great structure in order to look upon it at all hours of the day and night. They had something in common, and yet they could not have been more different. When Jim Wilcox approached Camus, the French man was pleased to share information on his favorite subject. But at first he did not understand that the history of Mont Saint Michel, like the structure itself, could become a part of an obsession in his guest. Camus sat back in his wicker chair, tapped his pipe, and filled it carefully with tobacco, as he prepared to tell Jim his favorite story:

"The origin of Mont Saint Michel grips the imagination, as does its harrowing history. In the sixth century on the coast of Normandy, there were two hermits named Paternus and S. Scubilion who took possession of two sites that were not covered by water at high tide. In Roman times, the rock and earth that rose out of the sea was known as Mons Jovis and was still connected to the mainland by a road surrounded by the Forest of Scissy. Actually there were two prominences—the larger one was called Mons Tumba and the smaller one was Tumbella. In 708 A.D. there was either a great flood or a tidal wave or a progressive erosion which devastated the land and left two mounds surrounded by water.

"At that time, the bishop of Avranches was directed in a series of dreams that he must build a sanctuary on the larger mound, Mons Tumba, in honor of the Archangel Michael. Latin descriptions state that the building was made in the form of a round crypt able to accommodate one hundred men. After the death of Charlemagne in 814 A.D., the raids by the Northmen were devastating, but the Mount survived and was eventually taken over by the Benedictines."

James Wilcox listened to these words as they became etched in that compartment of his brain which housed the great ambition.

For him this was no casual history lesson—it was a passionate experience from which he wanted to generate his chef d'oeuvres. Wilcox kept urging the French historian to keep talking. Jean Camus also loved the Mount, but he was not frantic about it, so he would casually light his pipe again and continue the tale:

"There were many fires at Mont Saint Michel, often started by lightning and fanned by the winds from the ocean. Each time the monks began to build again. Much of the base on the north side was built about 1106 to 1122. The stone arch that the King passed under when he came to visit became known as the Porte Du Roi. From 1191 to 1212, an Abbot named Jourdain directed the principal construction at Mont Saint Michel which included a number of buildings on the north side facing the sea. This façade became known as La Merveille because it was truly a fusion of nature and human inspiration!

"The continued building of the edifice was made possible in part because the reign of King John in England was coming to an end, and the attacks of the Norman Kings of England came to a close. There were many other structures added including the Salle des Chevaliers and a refectory later called the Salle des Hôtes. In the 13th century, the Châtelet, or gatehouse, was added, with its massive round towers. The magnificent Cloister was built from 1220-1228. It had two parallel ranges of columns and arches which alternated, or overlapped each other, and were connected by diagonal ribs. It is one of the most perfect Gothic works of its kind."

James Wilcox sat with his eyes riveted upon his host because he wanted to master every detail in this story. It was all destined to become part of his own ambition and the new architecture that he would create.

Jean Camus even introduced the legends that swirled around Mont Saint Michel:

"There are all kinds of marvelous stories and legends about the Mount," he said. "An old custom of the Mount was that no one should enter the church at night because the angels were said to meet there at night and sing, and their effulgence would cause any straggler to die within a few days."

That legend haunted James Wilcox, and his face gradually assumed a haggard expression. And yet as he left France, his eyes sparkled because he had found the great secret that he had searched for all his life—the genius of uniting a great natural wonder with human inspiration. His immediate task would be to find a majestic natural wonder in America, something super-natural, something made by the hand of God. Then he, himself, could superimpose an architectural creation of his own—that was the only way to consummate the superlative achievement that had escaped him so long.

For three years, Wilcox went about America working at a feverish pace to locate and study outstanding natural wonders in Arizona, Colorado, Nevada and Montana; then he located others in Maine, in New Hampshire, and in the Adirondacks. For each of these, he made measurements, tested materials, drew sketches, and created mock-ups and models. Finally, his partner Ed didn't like the pace that Wilcox had set for himself. All these trips, all these plans, all these details on top of the regular work duties were too much for anyone to bear. The whole obsession was obvi-ous to his partner Ed who began to view it as a sickness; and yet he had to admit that the great geniuses of history had all borne similar traits of obsessive fascination with a single purpose. So, even he began to believe in the wondrous architecture to come.

It might all have been a preamble to great success except for one thing. The more time went by, the more Ed recognized that James Wilcox was unable to produce a final plan. Instead, he kept searching for new avenues, incessantly making new dia-grams and waking up at night with new ideas which he then rejected a few days later. It really was a sickness, and Ed finally decided that he must talk with Jim about it again, even if it wore thin upon their friendship:

"You've made great progress," Ed began soothingly. "Your notion of combining a great natural wonder with a great creation of the human mind is unquestionably provocative."

Ed thought that would take the stress off Jim's face, but it did not. That was the sinister thing. No matter what encouragement was given, Jim still looked like a pent-up source of energy ready to explode, ready to unravel. So Ed continued:

"You've made such progress that I think you should take a month off and just relax. Then you could get back to it more effectively."

Wilcox grasped upon one part of the suggestion—the wrong part:

"You're right. I will take a month off and go to France. I'll go back to Mont Saint Michel, and when I see it again, now that I have dozens of possible plans, I'll be able to focus on the final one."

Ed was not so sure about the outcome of this trip, but he could see that there was no holding Jim back. Ed knew that James's obsession with the details of every activity at Mont Saint Michel was not quite normal, but even he had not understood how the place had attached itself to James's ambition and engulfed him. Ed hoped that travel might be better than all that theory, all that preoccupation with greatness. So they planned their office schedules so that Jim could set off, returning to the great symbol of all his aspirations!

In early June, Wilcox flew to France and quickly set out for Normandy. He took lodgings on the mainland overlooking the bay with Mont Saint Michel in full view. This way he had a good perspective, and he immediately set about filling in his information about the great structure by spending more time with Jean Camus. It was interesting to watch them together. Camus, always relaxed, seemed to bask in the glow of Mont Saint Michel, while Wilcox sat or stood like a coiled spring, waiting for the next word or the next visit to the great place.

Camus filled in more and more information—he spun it like a never-ending spider's web. And the ambition that drove James Wilcox caused him to be caught like a fly upon that spider's web, and he would flail around wildly, but uselessly.

One day Camus looked more somber when he spoke:

"There is a darker side to the Merveille, you know," he said with some hesitation, as he looked searchingly at his American friend. Wilcox was not dissuaded. He remained eager to learn everything, no matter what it was, so Camus continued:

"Louis XV imprisoned Victor de la Castagne (known as Dubourg) in the so-called iron cage in the prisons of the cellar. Dubourg, a gazetteer of Holland, had displeased the King, and he was placed in the iron cage which had walls actually made of stone and timbers. The cage was about twenty feet high and only twelve feet square. Dubourg was forced to live in this cage all alone for a year, and he died raving mad in 1746.

"There were other terrible events at Mont Saint Michel, as well as acts of heroism. There was a large wheel, or poulain, which operated to draw up water from the well below. Prisoners were made to walk inside the great wheel for hours, using human sweat and pain to make it turn and pull up casks of water. In 1591, this wheel system almost served as the means for an invasion by the Huguenots. There was a traitor to the Mount named Goupigny who might have caused the capture of the place, but he was a double agent and also a traitor to his Huguenot friends outside. Owing to his treachery, eighty Huguenots who had made it up the rope were butchered at the top. Their friends were waiting below for some sign from above and received what appeared to be the body of a dead monk— actually it was the body of one of their own men who had been dressed in a robe. At this point, the would-be invaders below did not know what to do, so they chose to send up a single man named Rablotière. When he arrived at the top, he was also taken prisoner and almost butchered on the spot. Instead, he was offered his life if he would betray his Huguenot friends below and call out to them that all was well. And now came one of the great moments of heroism of all time. Rablotière, surrounded by his enemies, came to the top of the shaft and screamed down a single word, 'Treachery!'"

Jean Camus paused, watching the effect of his tale upon his guest. Camus saw beads of sweat on Jim's forehead, so he tried to present a more cheerful side of the story:

"The redeeming part of this event was that the commander of The Mount, the governor, was so impressed with Rablotière's courage that he spared his life."

Camus paused again, but only for a moment, because he would not hide the truth. He kept feeding information into his ravenous guest, depicting the evils that haunted the great structure.

"The sinister aspects of Mont Saint Michel continued during the Terror of the French Revolution when hundreds of monks were brought there against their will. Later, in 1811, Napoleon turned the place into a house of correction, and many miserable human beings suffered in its cellars until it ceased to be a prison in 1863."

Camus was unwittingly provoking Wilcox into a frenzy by following every story with a succeeding tale, as if they would never end:

"Over the years, there were many pilgrims, monks, and cavalry drowned on their trips or approaches to the Mount because of the forty-foot tides that sweep in around it so rapidly. People got caught again and again because the treacherous tide doesn't come in a straight line, but flows in rapidly like so many newly formed rivers encircling its victims.

"One cannot deny that Mont Saint Michel has some of the most beautiful structures in the world. But one must also admit that it is a place where nature has killed hundreds of human beings, and worse yet, where men have created terror in the hearts of other human beings and brought unbearable pain to their bodies."

With this news, Wilcox could not deny the dark side of the underbelly of the structure that he had idolized! Now, with his idealized dreams of perfect beauty shattered, he should have turned away from the Mount and the Merveille, but he could not. Wilcox, consumed by his obsession, was instead gripped by all its aspects, as if caught in the iron cage himself.

Wilcox became surrounded by an eerie atmosphere in which the architecture of the Mount, its glorious and terrifying history, and his own efforts to be creative began to cycle incessantly in his mind. The French man sensed that all was not well in the mind of his guest and tried to warn him:

"You seem to have set yourself up in competition with Mont Saint Michel, as if you would overcome it and create something greater," he mused. "You must remember that these great structures and their history march inexorably forward, but human beings are not like that. We survive by being more flexible, by giving in a little here and there. If we don't do that, we get crushed like a bug."

Wilcox hesitated for an instant, but he did not really hear him. His mind was at fever pitch, and he determined that he must get closer yet to the beauty and the terror of Mont Saint Michel! To do that, he chose to actually live within its walls, taking quarters in one of those ancient stone houses that line the cobblestone streets around the base of the famous structure. To find such a place, he walked through the streets, asking people where he might find a room. Finally, someone told him about an old woman who managed a rental. After meeting her, he just followed the directions that she gave him.

First he walked down one of those narrow cobblestone streets—a street barely wide enough for a single car and lined by stone buildings which reeked of ages past. Wilcox truly felt that he was entering into the past. He wondered how many monks, courtiers, knights, soldiers, pilgrims, prisoners, and others, with hope in their hearts and misery in their future, might have walked these streets. He looked at the ancient ramparts and wondered how many frightened soldiers had defended its walls and shed their blood into these same streets, onto the same stones on which he walked.

Wilcox reached the door to which he had been directed, holding in his hand the large and ancient key the woman had given him. He stared at the building's ancient stones and timbers. A large iron lock accepted the key that he held tightly in his hand. The entrance was dark, but it led into two rooms with old rugged furniture. There was a bed and a dresser with a wash basin and a pitcher full of clear water. One bar of soap and a towel hung nearby. The old chairs had gnarled wooden legs and arms, and a few tapestries hung on the walls.

But it was the window of the room that caught the attention of James Wilcox. The window frame was constructed of blocks of granite, and the window itself had colored glass set in lead frames. The window hung by iron hinges, and when Wilcox swung it open, he knew that he had come to the right place. He could look down to the narrow winding streets, the parapets and the towers, and beyond the ramparts to the barren sand. Wilcox had finally managed to move his life inside the architecture, as if he had been swallowed by it. He looked out of the window, as if he were a part of the ancient structure, as if he were one of the ancient people who had passed this way or lived here and died.

Suddenly as he looked down upon the sand, he saw something far away, far out toward the ocean of the choppy channel sea. There, he perceived a strange sight, as if there were something churning at the distant edge of the shore. The tide had turned, and the great waters of the ocean were moving in to surround Mont Saint Michel and himself. Like the water from a broken dam, it flowed with amazing speed toward the shore. Sometimes in sheets of water, and elsewhere like newly formed rivers, the waters came. With great force, the water raced toward the land, as if it hoped to catch one more unsuspecting victim, as it had hundreds of times in the past. And the rivulets that came and circled in complicated patterns were like tentacles that reached beyond the main body that followed. Within a short time as night came, the waters rose around the isolated Mount, trying once more to engulf everything in its path—it was an awesome scene as the forty-foot tide rushed in with the darkness.

Wilcox, tired from his incessant pursuit of information, decided he must turn into bed. But when the lights were off, he could not stop listening to the sounds of the sea beating upon the rocks surrounding Mont Saint Michel, and once again he conjured up all those hundreds of architectural plans that he had started. At first it was a form of intense pleasure for him, but gradually as darkness set in more and more, the vision of those plans began to spin within his mind. He could lie still no longer and suddenly jumped up to look again from that stone-arched window at the sands below. There was just enough light remaining for him to see the grotesque shapes of buildings, and there was a surging of the sea with foam beneath the rising moon. Wilcox forced himself to return to his bed, but he could not stop listening.

Suddenly, there was an eerie call, repeated over and over again. It was like a scream of ancient pain. At first, Wilcox could not place it, but it had a mournful sound and seemed to come from the air above his window and out toward the water's edge. Finally, he saw a shadow sweep past his window and recognized the wings of a great gull. Soon there were many gulls sweeping back and forth and landing periodically to grasp some unlucky shell fish that was stranded near the edge of the water. The whole eerie scene was causing the idealistic image that Wilcox had formed of the Mount to unravel rapidly. The great hope he had formed the first time he saw the beauty of Mont Saint Michel was now mixed with the reality before him and the horror of its history. All of Wilcox's hopes for a project full of beauty seemed to come apart before him. He tried to make himself sleep, but the mournful calls continued, and Wilcox developed a thought that screamed at his very essence. Half-awake and half-asleep, he was sure that the gulls he heard must be the actual descendants of gulls long ago which flew by the windows and were heard by the poor souls imprisoned in the cellar of Mont Saint Michel—those poor devils who lived within the Iron Cage until they could stand it no longer, and their sanity escaped where they could not.

The next day, visitors at Mont Saint Michel were surprised to hear the sirens of police cars. A man was carried away in some kind of restraining camisole.

No one knew what had happened, but the following day there was a short newsclip in one of the French newspapers. The newsclip announced that an American architect had been found wandering about the cobblestone streets in his pajamas, apparently stark raving mad. He clutched a mass of drawings in his hands and rushed to the parapets where he threw them into the sea. Each time a map floated through the air to the sands and the water, a gull would swoop down to see if it was something to eat—there was soon a flurry of papers landing on the swirling waters below and making strange floating patterns on the surface. Visitors had been amazed at the sight and called the police who responded, as they always do, by dragging away the disheveled man.

It was the end of a chapter, the end of one man's life. But Mont Saint Michel went on, as it always does, and soon all the foreign visitors settled back to their pleasures—meeting the guides who led them about to see the beauty of the Merveille, the double arches of the magnificent cloister, the imposing rooms, and the cellar with its human cages which evinced frightful memories. The gulls still swooped about the air and the beaches, calling forth with those voices from the past.

THE BETTER SIDE

He was a piggy little man with slit-like eyes, and he was the manager of the suburban department store, so he controlled the lives of countless people who worked there. Overbeak was one of those people who spent his life getting the most work out of other people without doing much himself. His constant fidgeting and rushing about convinced the president of the department store chain that he was the best manager he could get. When employees complained—only a few had ever dared—Overbeak had a way of disarming them by the way he talked with the president, Mr. Witherman:

"I'll admit to you, Mr. Witherman, that I'm very exacting, but my philosophy is that I'm not here to make friends; I'm here to make the most efficient work force and save as much salary money as possible."

On this lofty basis, Overbeak could indulge himself in chastising employees without mercy. They put up with it because salaries were higher than in any other stores in town. Mr. Witherman didn't like Overbeak's approach, but he tolerated anything that cut down expenditures and maximized profit. Then too, Overbeak was always agreeable in Mr. Witherman's presence, so the boss never actually witnessed the harassment.

Perhaps employees exaggerated, he thought.

When Annabelle was hired, the other workers were worried about her right away. She was such a sweet and vulnerable little thing that they knew immediately that she was a perfect victim for Overbeak. Several people tried to warn her:

"Don't feel hurt when he yells at you, never trust him, and act a little tough, or he will run all over you," they said.

Annabelle listened, but it was not the kind of advice she was able to take. Because her constitution was incapable of aggression, she had generated a philosophy of life to match:

"I always find that people show the best side of their nature when I just act nice to them. My mother always said, 'You can get more out of people with sugar than...'"

She couldn't even finish the sentence before Will Granger interrupted:

"Honey, this just isn't the kind of man you can do that with."

Annabelle persisted with her good family's teachings:

"I think everybody has a good side, a better side."

The other salespeople gave up and just waited apprehensively to see what would happen to the poor girl.

It wasn't long in coming. Overbeak hounded her from the start. He had an instinct for brutalizing people he knew would be too timid to complain to the president's office. Every time he harassed her, she responded with her nervous apologies, her gentle smile.

When other workers tried to console her and urged her to stand up to him, she would say:

"If I stay nice, he'll change someday."

The weeks passed, the months went by, and after more than two years, the pattern of harassment went on unabated.

The only hope for Annabelle was that she found a friend to talk to. It was an odd match. Her new friend was a boy hired to carry the heavy boxes and move furniture and anything else that needed muscle. And muscles he had! They bulged out on his arms and in his neck and in the calves of his legs. Roy was a tough kid who grew up near the elevated in New York. He had the usual accent, and he didn't have much use for anybody in the fancy store, except that he took a liking to Annabelle. He told her she was sweet, the way his sister was before she died. When Overbeak tried to bulldoze Roy, he got a reaction he wasn't used to. Roy turned a sullen look toward him and said:

"Hey man, I'm doin' my job."

Everybody thought Roy would be fired on the spot, but it didn't happen. It was as if Mr. Overbeak were a little afraid of him. Instead of firing him, Overbeak redoubled his harassment of everybody else, and of course Annabelle.

Poor Annabelle was pretty discouraged by now. She held tightly to her belief in the good side of people because it was the only reaction she was able to muster. She persisted in her sweet, nervous responses, but it was beginning to wear her down. She was pale and losing weight. People advised her to quit.

"I can't do that," she said plaintively. "My father's out of work and my mother's sick. I'm the only one with a salary, the only support they've got. I can't take any chances on losing our only income. I tried to find another job, but I couldn't."

She didn't even know that when other stores sent letters of inquiry about her to Overbeak, he just buried the letters.

"Don't keep giving Overbeak as a reference," the others told her. "There's no telling what he may say."

Annabelle couldn't believe that:

"He may be grumpy," she said, "but he wouldn't just make things up." She still believed in that better side.

Just when all Annabelle's co-workers were about to give up on it all, a strange thing happened. Mr. Overbeak came in one day with a harried expression. He was jumpy and restless. Of course, he still harangued everyone he came to, but there was one exception. Whenever he came to Annabelle's counter, he tried to smile—which was very difficult for him.

The girl at the next counter noticed it right away, and soon everybody in the store knew about it. They were so amazed that everybody whispered about it at all the water fountains and during lunch:

"Did you hear about Annabelle and Mr. Overbeak?" they would ask.

And the answers were all over the place. Some said they were suspicious that he had become interested in her as a woman and went as far as to suggest that she might be having an affair with him. But that seemed so repulsive that most people rejected the idea. Others recalled how Annabelle had always said she could bring out the best in people, and a few actually began to believe in her philosophy, at least a little. Finally, they talked to her about it, and she responded in the only way she could. She was even more surprised than they were at the happy turn of events, but to explain it she could only muster up her beautiful belief in trust and the goodness of other people:

"Even Mr. Overbeak," she said, "must have a better side. Of course, I have to admit that I almost gave up on him. But my mother always said, 'Just be yourself, and everything will be all right.'"

There was no question about the complete change in Overbeak's treatment of one of his victims. But it was positively grotesque, the way Overbeak made that weird effort to smile when he came by Annabelle's counter. It came out as a strange crooked smile, and it was so extraordinary that rumors to explain it continued to multiply. It was obvious that Mr. Overbeak had no change in his attitude toward anybody else, so people had become convinced that it must be something special about Annabelle's outlook on life. Gradually the cynical outlook decreased, and many people accepted a more optimistic outlook upon human nature—after all, Annabelle's goodness had changed the heart of a man who had never shown any signs of compassion.

No one could believe what they were all seeing! It remained the talk of the store, and no one fully understood it except Mr. Overbeak, and he wouldn't talk.

Only one other person ever found out part of the real story, and that was Mr. Overbeak's secretary, Miss Hazelworth. She had seen Mr. Overbeak's frenzied look on the morning when his whole attitude changed. As he came into the office, she expressed concern:

"You look terrible, Mr. Overbeak," she said, "Are you all right?"

Tight-lipped, he mumbled:

"I'm all right, but I don't know what this neighborhood is coming to. Last night, right in the parking lot of the store, I was grabbed and roughed up by a masked man who handed me a threatening note. I never saw his face. I'm afraid the big city has come to the suburbs."

"Did he threaten you for money?" Miss Hazelworth had asked.

"No," said Overbeak, "just a general threatening note. People don't care what they do to others anymore."

As Overbeak took off his overcoat, a small piece of paper dropped to the ground. Miss Hazelworth ignored it, but after he went out of the office, she picked it up to throw it in the waste basket. Just as she was about to toss it, she noticed some handwriting on it, and since it was just a piece of paper from the floor, she thought she was entitled to look at it.

The handwriting was awkward, and the spelling was bad, but the message was clear:

Hey Man, Leave Annabelle alone, or I'll beat ya to
a bloody pulp. Call the Cops and you is dead.

This would have been big news for the gossip mills of the store, but Miss Hazelworth decided not to say anything. She was afraid for her job, and she thought Mr. Overbeak might figure out who found the note.

Life at the store in the suburbs continued much the same after that, except that Mr. Overbeak was very nice to Annabelle. At Christmas time, Annabelle said a prayer at her church for Mr. Overbeak, and she even brought a little present for him. When he thanked her with that crooked smile, everyone began to think that Annabelle was right after all—about bringing out the man's better side.

THE HOUSE OF SHADOWS

The house was a veritable castle built of large rocks. It was perched at the top of a slope, gracefully astride the highest part of the meadow that surrounded it. The handsome building even vaunted a small tower that dominated the countryside. There were a few sculptured figures along the eaves that put one in mind of gargoyles—human and animal heads. The massive grandeur and the austerity of the structure were never so prominent as on summer evenings when the shadows of the tower and the eaves of the house put forth strange shapes along the ground that reached far down the surrounding meadow. Small herds of deer grazed in the meadow, but when the deer walked toward the house, they always stopped about halfway up the field, as if their senses warned them not to approach too close—as if a second sense told them that all was not well inside.

It was different at the lower end of the meadow where Alice Wentworth, a young teen-ager, and her family had moved into a very expensive modern home. Alice used to stare toward the house at the top of the hill to catch a glimpse of anyone coming or going. But she had never seen a soul, only a long black car that left each morning and came back in the late afternoon. Alice

watched the shadows cast by the great house, and it was she who
called it "The House of Shadows."

When Alice's first winter in her new house was passed and
spring came, the surrounding houses released their occupants to
work in the gardens and the fields. But the great stone house
maintained its quiet isolation, its closed doors and windows, and
its atmosphere of separation from the rest of the world.

Alice and her school classmate, Joan, used to sit and stare at
the great house on the hill:

"It looks weird," Joan would say. "Are you going to tell me
that someone was murdered there?"

Alice's older brother, Ralph, would join in:

"I don't think anybody lives there at all. It's just a front."

Then he entertained the girls by saying that it was the center
of a drug ring, and that it was run by the Mafia.

"The house is just a drop-off place," he would say, as he
elaborated upon the black car that came and went.

That idea made everyone laugh, and often, Mr. and Mrs.
Wentworth would join recklessly into the fun, extending their
sarcasm to the weird people who never appeared. Mr. Wentworth
proposed, with much humor, that it was a house of prostitution
because he thought he had seen a few fancy women in cars in front
of the house. Whether those women had anything to do with the
inhabitants was never determined. Mrs. Wentworth was less
amused by the whole thing, not because she had any concern for
the people who lived inside, but because she worried that if they
were unsavory people, they might be of some risk to her family:

"What if it were the central hideout for a gang, and they were
raided by the FBI, and everybody started shooting?" she would
ask.

Whenever Alice invited her friend Joan, the Wentworths
readily drew her into making fun of "The House of Shadows"
and its inhabitants. Joan went along, but the relentless humor
made her uncomfortable.

One day Alice climbed to the top of the hill and walked all around the house. She even looked in the windows. She had been scolded for that, but it didn't keep her parents from asking:

"What did you see?"

"I saw the living room," said Alice, "with its dark curtains partly closed and lots of heavy-looking furniture. It was dark inside, so I couldn't really make anything out very well, but there was a person!"

The Wentworths had jumped at that:

"What was the person like?"

Alice enjoyed the questions and took her time answering:

"At one side of the room there was a large reclining chair and in it was a woman. She was all wrapped up in a blanket, and she just sat very still. She was surrounded by figures which at first I thought were people, but then I realized that they were mannequins. As the evening sun went through the house, the shadows of the mannequins moved slowly on the window panes. I got scared, so I ran away."

Another day Alice claimed she had seen a man—he was a big man with a brimmed hat and a big coat, and he had driven up to the front of the old house in the black limousine. He unlocked the front door and went inside. Alice had the nerve to creep over to one of the side windows. Later, when she got home, she described what she had seen. She told her family that she had seen the man in the living room looming over the woman in the chair. He had a little bottle, and he poured a dark liquid into a teaspoon and gave it to the woman. Alice's imagination was pretty good, so the Wentworths were not sure how much truth there was in it. But they were ready to believe, and they all added their own interpretations regarding the house and its occupants.

The mystery of "The House of Shadows" was no longer a matter of observation, but one of a growing set of assumptions regarding the people inside, people who dared to live without relating to their neighbors.

During the next few years, the Wentworths' own house became a great estate as Mr. Wentworth earned a lot of money and hired a contractor to make an enormous addition, including a swimming pool. Mrs. Wentworth ordered the construction of a barn, and she bought horses. Landscapers were always outside converting the field into tiers separated by paths and decorative rocks. So in time, visitors made repeated comparisons of the Wentworth estate and the castle at the top of the hill. But no matter what the Wentworths did to aggrandize their property, they could not give it the impressive allure that the great castle-like house had in such abundance.

Of course, the Wentworths had great social events at their house, inviting many influential people. Whenever anyone commented upon the castle at the top of the hill, Mrs. Wentworth put on a supercilious look so that none of her guests would mistakenly believe that she associated with the owners. The children followed suit. And it was obvious that the great structure at the top of the hill was ill-kept, clearly not thriving with new money. Mrs. Wentworth often described how the inhabitants remained hidden inside. Still, in some ways, the castle remained more impressive than the Wentworth house, or the homes of any of their guests. In time, the comments regarding the owners became more and more intemperate. The Wentworths and other neighbors were especially critical of the woman in the old house because she had made no effort to meet other women—no exchange of information, no small talk, no effort to please. And the ladies all concluded from her reclusive nature that she must not care about anybody else.

The mystery of the old house, the aloofness of its inhabitants, and the unkempt nature of the place mixed with its unrelenting impressiveness. There was by now an open hostility to all that, and Alice and her brother were a part of it merely because they were growing up with it. But no matter what the Wentworths and their friends did, and no matter what they said, they could not match the grandeur from above. They could not have hated the place and the people who lived inside more if they had really known anything about them, so they reacted by having larger and larger social events, as if to overwhelm the place.

Alice was a part of it all by default. And yet during all the important events at the Wentworth's house, there were moments when Alice sat alone in her room, or sought out a nook in the kitchen where she could be herself. She could circulate among her parents' guests, but gradually she became aware that if she moved away to her room, no one noticed or cared. And one day she experienced a twinge of uncertainty, almost like a short sharp pain in her side, when she heard the adults go so far as to speculate about organizing a petition to have the old house declared an eyesore. This might lead to having it taken down at some point in the future. It was the first time that Alice really stepped back from the mass of guests in her own home, and even from her own family.

At another time, Alice also noticed that when her mother spoke with friends, it was mostly to pick up personal information that she could pass on to others. But one day as Alice and Joan listened to such a conversation, Joan put it bluntly:

"Our mothers are always gossiping," she said.

And finally there was a more meaningful day when Alice walked in upon a violent argument between her mother and father—there was something vile about the way they spoke to each other. Alice ran off to her own room and, looking out the window at "The House of Shadows," she thought for a moment that it seemed more peaceful there. Still, the very fancy modern house in which Alice and her parents lived and the beautiful landscaping all spoke for the established success of her family and herself. Alice could see that most of her neighbors considered her and her family to be upper-class. Success spoke for itself.

It was different after Alice graduated from high school and went away to college. Far from her own home, surrounded by peers and professors, she became a part of a new world. And once in a while, when she thought about home, or when she came back on vacation, she looked at her parents through a different glass. And she experienced more and more doubts about what she had grown up with. Eventually, though, she too might well have gone back to her parents' ways, except for a letter that showed up in her mailbox at the dorm—the letter was from her mother, and it had two shocking messages!

The first message was that her father and mother were separating. Of course Alice's mother put the best face upon it, and she explained at length that when two people are not getting along it makes sense for them to live apart. Perhaps, but it was still a shock! It meant that Alice had no house to go home to. Alice may have been partly prepared by years of foreboding—by a child's understanding through unexpressed feeling. But she now felt very much alone. A college dormitory was fun when you had a home base, but it was a cold place when there was nothing else. Alice cried.

The second message of the letter was not about her own family, and yet, in a strange way, it hit Alice the hardest. It referred to an article in a local newspaper, and a copy of the article was enclosed. It had been given to Mrs. Wentworth by Alice's friend, Joan, and it was obvious that Mrs. Wentworth had not read it. The newspaper clipping was a short editorial from a local paper. It described an event in her home town—a human interest story. The full text by the reporter was included:

OLD COUPLE DIES AFTER LONG SIEGE

Many people in town never saw them, but they were here among us. All of you have seen the old house at the top of the East hill, the one built of stone and dominated by a turret. But, until now, no one ever knew what transpired inside.

There was an old couple, the Dudleys, who lived inside those walls. Married for almost fifty years, they had a single child, a little blond girl who suddenly developed a fever at the age of nine. At first, they thought it was just a cold, but within twelve hours she was desperately sick and soon lapsed into a coma. There was talk of meningitis and encephalitis. A couple of days later, she was dead!

The mother never recovered from the loss of her only child, and she reacted by locking herself up in the great house. For forty years the husband cared for his wife, sacrificing every other aspect of his life. For forty years he went off in the car to work, and each day he returned as soon as he could, to wait on her, to feed her, to help her dress, to give her medicine, and to envelop her with all the love that he could muster, while struggling for survival. From time to time, Mrs. Dudley improved enough to work a little at her old trade—she was a seamstress and made custom clothes that she made to fit on the many mannequins that she kept in the house. There was only a little money from her work, but if her husband could sell one of the dresses she made, it helped him pay the taxes on their ancient home.

The quiet struggle for survival behind the stone walls of the old house, with barely enough money for subsistence, explain why the couple was never seen around town or on the street. They had no friends, and they had no entertainment, but they had each other.

One day last week the old man and his wife were found dead in their living room. She was lying in her chair, and he was on the floor in front of her with one hand holding on to one of her feet. The coroner reported an extraordinary thing. He said that they died within a few hours of each other, and yet there was no evidence of foul play, nor any evidence of suicide. Apparently, she died first, and he died soon after, as if he had just been waiting for her to go first.

There was always controversy about the old house since some people thought it was an eyesore. Someone, disregarding the people living inside, even made up a cruel name for the old structure and called it "The House of Shadows." But a number of architects believe that the structure is unique, and a fund has been started to mark the old house for historic preservation in view of its architecture and the personal legend that seems to be growing about the old couple who lived so much alone and died at the same time.

Alice crumpled the little article in her tightening grip. She was motionless. She knew that it was she, herself, who had first called it "The House of Shadows."

Alice now felt no pleasure in college life, and she did not know whether to attach herself to one parent or the other, or to separate herself from them both.

At the end of the semester, Alice decided that she must visit her old neighborhood, even though her parents were no longer living there—it would be a pilgrimage. She felt a compulsion to go there, to see it, to experience it again, to find something of herself there. But when she got there, she did not go to her own house. Instead, her feet moved nervously to the little road that led to the house at the top of the hill. That was what she had come for! She looked again at the heavy stones that made up the walls of the old house; she felt them with her hand to experience the heat of the sun that they retained; and then she walked slowly around the whole house, passing from the sunlight into the shadows cast by the turret, and again into the rays of the sun. Alice looked at the panes of glass in the old windows with their bluish tinge, but she did not go forward to look inside. Alice felt that there was something sacred there, something powerful.

Eventually, Alice's feet led her slowly down the meadow to a point midway between the great old house and the home she had lived in, and there she paused again to look at one house and then at the other. And as she looked up the hill, she could no longer imagine what it was that had made her family laugh at the old stone place. The austerity that Alice had seen or imagined in the past gave way to stateliness. The stone walls stood steadily against the wind, and the turret reached strongly toward the sky. As the old stone house above took on the evening's glow, there were reddish hues that reflected the warmth inside. And as the sun set deeper in the West, the rays came through the old house, forming beautiful golden reflections in its window panes.

Alice walked slowly away through the meadow between the two houses, and she knew that the shadows up above, and those down below, would never quite fade away.

A few months later, there was a conversation at the local newspaper office. The editor of the paper was speaking to one of the reporters:

"I'm sure you're aware of the historic preservation fund initiated by local architects after they read our editorial about the old castle on the hill. They're getting many large donations. It's amazing how much latent interest there was in that place. Some people are fascinated by the ancient architecture, and others by the love story inside that was ignored so long. Business people want to use the place to attract tourism. I think it's going to become a legend."

The reporter agreed and added one thing more:

"Just this morning, I heard about an interesting donation that came in an unmarked envelope. There were five hundred dollars inside, all in cash, with a little card suggesting that the place should be called "The Dudley Castle" in honor of the last people to live there. The gift was essentially anonymous—it was just signed "Alice.""

DIVERSITY

Alfred Winslow ran the printing presses at the Harrison and Tucker Press, but he knew there was very little future in it unless he could start a business of his own. He felt confident about his skills with the presses since he not only ran them personally, but knew a lot about their maintenance and repairs. Alfred had a little money saved to invest in a printing business of his dreams, but deep inside himself, he knew that he lacked "the business sense." What if he invested his money and lost it all! The uncertainty and the fear had always kept Alfred under somebody else's thumb, and he was not happy about that. Yet, he could not quite see a safe way out of the box he was in. His wife Millie and their daughter Anna wanted him to stay where he was—it was safe.

"Sure it's safe," Alfred would yell at Millie in exasperation, "but I'm going exactly nowhere."

"Nowhere is better than the street," Millie would answer.

"Stuck, stuck, stuck," he would call back.

They really got on very well together, but this was a sore issue.

One day on a bus trip, they happened to start talking to a man and his wife. The man was Abe Rosenblum, his wife was

Sarah, and they had a nineteen-year-old son called Lester.

When Alfred and Millie got home, he turned to her:

"That guy Rosenblum knows a lot about small business management. If I got him into the printing business with me, we could combine my know-how with his and open up our own printing establishment."

"Would you want to have him as a business partner?"

"I need someone like that to get me out of working for someone else."

"Yeah," said Millie, "but would you trust him? That type is all right as an acquaintance, but I'm not sure about putting our money in with him. Could you get along with him?"

"I guess we'd have to find that out," responded Alfred.

"We'd have to put up half the money," said Millie, looking doubtful again.

They argued about that for a while, but finally agreed to look into it. Alfred called Abe, discussed the whole thing on the phone, and then met with him and Sarah, who looked just as doubtful as Millie. After much agonizing, they took the plunge.

They rented space, bought equipment on credit, and started in. It was a winning combination. Abe knew how to do the advertising and public relations, and Alfred was a good printer. They were soon getting orders and filling them. It was ideal from the point of view of skills, but there was one nagging trouble—they didn't fully trust each other. And there was no help from Millie or Sarah, who added to the suspicion. They had nothing against each other personally—it was just that they came from such different backgrounds. Alfred and Millie would not admit they were anti-Semitic, but when they said they couldn't quite trust people like that with money, it was pretty obvious what they meant. Abe and Sarah knew how often Christians had never quite accepted them, so they remained skeptical too. Still, they were all making more money than ever before, and that kept the prejudices and doubts subdued.

One year later, with rapid growth, Alfred decided they needed a full-time accountant:

"I know a guy from my old office who might be enticed to join us," he told Abe.

"Great," said Abe. "What's his name?"

"He's called Ahrad. I never knew the rest of his name; everyone just called him Ahrad. He's very good with numbers and records."

Suddenly, Abe was a little cooler on the subject, but they agreed that Alfred should at least talk to him. Ahrad was excited about the possibility because he also wanted to be a full partner in something and not just an employee. Alfred had no objection to that.

Alfred came back to Abe with the great news, but Abe took a different attitude:

"I don't mind hiring the guy, but I don't want him as my partner."

Alfred proposed that they get to know him for a while before making a decision. They got Millie and Sarah to set up a few dinners so they could all meet Ahrad. Both Alfred and Millie thought the new man was just what they needed, and Millie saw a chance for an improved home life:

"You'll both be free of all that bookkeeping," Millie said. "Perhaps you can spend a little more time at home." Abe and Sarah were quiet. They raised hesitant objections, but when they were home alone, they said it bluntly:

"Of all the people in this city, they have to bring us an Arab!"

Abe and Sarah were fighting a losing battle because Ahrad was soon recommended as the best accountant they could find. They knew it was true, so they had to take him. However they tried again and again to bring him in as an employee. Ahrad was a quiet man, showing no signs of being demanding, but he was quietly fixed upon one idea. He wanted to join the group as a full member of the company, or he would not come. Finally, in spite of much reluctance on the part of Abe and Sarah, he was accepted.

As luck would have it, the editor of the town newspaper decided to write about the Winslow-Rosenblum-Ahrad printing business as an example of American success. The article featured the Christian printer, the Jewish businessman, and the Arab accountant as models of successful diversity.

What a team! What a success! The jobs kept rolling in because of Abe's advertising and the high quality of work that Alfred could produce. Ahrad sent out the bills, collected the money, did inventories, and made out all the tax forms. They were making more money than any of them had seen before, and they were expanding so fast that they had to rent an extra space halfway down the block and hire extra clerks. This kind of rapid success subverted any potential disagreements. The abundance of money was like a superior type of oil which kept everything running smoothly and kept suspicion in the background.

It might have gone on like this forever except that the children were growing up. Lester Rosenblum was now twenty-one, and Anna Winslow was eighteen. If they had fought with each other, everything would have been all right—the parents would have been good arbiters. The trouble came because they got along so well. They really liked each other from the start. Lester followed Anna around wherever she went, and Anna, far from resisting, encouraged him at every opportunity. Unlike their parents, they hadn't even thought about any ethnic differences which seemed like something out of the past to them. All Lester could see was a pretty blond girl with blue eyes and a soft disposition mingled with obvious natural intelligence. For her part, Anna liked to have Lester watch her with his dark intense eyes. She needed a young man who was bright and personally attentive—he was both. The physical chemistry was good, and beyond that, they had long philosophical discussions in which they agreed more than they argued. What could be better for the parents' relationships and the business than children who got on so well together? It turned out that ignoring each other would have been easier.

The first trouble came with the happiness of Christmas. Lester told his parents that he would spend Christmas Eve and most of Christmas Day at the Winslow's house, and he described to them what a happy event it would be. Sarah and Abe shook their heads in agreement, but then proceeded to describe all the lights and tinsel as gaudy. They also compared the occasion to their own religious holidays, pointing out that Christmas was a commercial venture, no longer a real religious holiday, if it had ever been one. Lester was a little shaken by this until he got to the Christmas celebration and found that, aside from gifts, the Winslows were in fact quite devoted to the real meaning of Christmas. Until this day, he had always thought prejudice was a Christian phenomenon. Anna strengthened her bond to Lester by telling him how her parents had hesitated to go into business with his parents, all for the wrong reasons. The young people felt closer together and more distant from their parents.

As the generations split, all the forces of trouble were mobilized. First there was the awkward way in which the Winslows behaved when they attended Bar Mitzvahs in the Rosenblums' extended family. Then, there was the inability of the Winslows to remember the Jewish Sabbath, their disregard for the dietary laws that the Rosenblums practiced, and their insensitivity to the importance of minority representation. In addition to that, there was the Rosenblums' steady pressure to hire Jewish workers at the business. They attributed their choices to the high skills of the candidates, but always came up with same result—it was like a network that made Alfred uncomfortable. In addition, Millie learned that the Rosenblums always voted for Jewish candidates in city elections.

Throughout all this, Ahrad was slightly amused at them. His

political views were more blatantly one-sided, so he never talked about them in the company of his business associates. All the dancing around that they did left him alternately perplexed or entertained.

Still, money was pouring into the business, and they opened another printing outfit on the other side of town. It was becoming a big operation, and that held everything together at work.

One day the kids, Lester and Anna, were hanging around at their parents' business after hours, and Ahrad happened to be working late. That led to a late afternoon conversation in which Ahrad was pretty direct, as usual:

"You two getting pretty interested in each other?" he asked.

It was the first time that the relationship had been openly discussed at the printing office. It didn't bother the kids at all, but it lead to their openly telling Ahrad about their parents' resistance to their liaison. They hinted strongly that they felt it was due to "the differences."

Ahrad looked at them seriously and gave his regular straight answer:

"I never found the woman I wanted, but if I did, I would marry her, no matter what anybody else thought."

When Sarah heard about this conversation, she was furious:

"It's one thing for him to be in this business with us; it's something else for him to mess with our children." Abe agreed and talked with Ahrad, even threatening to break up the partnership. It became a long argument, but in the end, the money held things together again.

When the kids decided to get married, there was a barrage of parental admonitions which had no effect, and finally the four parents had to give in, as always. The worst time came when Sarah, alone with Lester, raised one last telling objection to the marriage:

"In what religion are we going to raise your children?" she asked, thinking that there was no simple answer for her son to produce. Instead, Lester became very direct and cross enough to challenge his mother openly:

"There's nothing for you to trouble yourself with, Mom, because you're not going to raise the children; Millie and I are going to do it."

"You talk to your mother like that?" screamed Sarah.

It was the climax to the whole situation, the climax that had to come at some time. After that, mother and son settled into an armed truce. The wedding took place; the young couple took off for Acapulco. They actually considered living there, but eventually they came back home to finish college. After that, everyone was interested in knowing what Lester and Anna would do for a living. Anna was interested in the fashion world, and she was lucky enough to find a job away from the family. Poor Lester had always been fascinated by the idea of taking charge of the family printing presses. He had tinkered with the presses for years, the way other kids tinker with cars, and he had learned about computers and new electronic printing in school. But working in the family business meant adjusting to Alfred Winslow and also working for his own father. That meant getting embroiled in all the family problems. He told Ahrad about his problem. Ahrad could see that it was a problem, but he never gave an opinion because he had learned.

At first, Lester wouldn't even talk about working for his father. But after he went around looking at other jobs where they wanted to give him an entry-level position, he decided to stay on in the family business.

What a group! They had a Jewish-Christian problem, a Jewish-Arab problem, a mixed religion marriage, and a potential explosion when future grandchildren made their appearance. Looking at it from the outside, the owner of the furniture store next to the printing establishment was the only one who could look at it objectively. Paul Solomon was a wise old businessman, and he would talk to his wife Sadie about it:

"If I had to invent a new cocktail that no one could drink, I would put all those people into it together," he would say.

Sadie, who kept the accounts in their store, looked at it from a business standpoint:

"They're doin' awfully good; the fastest growing business in town."

Paul would nod his head in agreement, then shake it slowly from side to side while lowering the sides of his mouth:

"It's a strong business, all right," he would say, "like a nuclear bomb. But how's it going to end? Nothing can bring peace over there."

Sadie insisted on her optimistic business view:

"You know what it is they've got over there? It's what they call diversity. That's what made this country great."

Paul remained skeptical:

"They've certainly got diversity, and that may be what made America great, but a little downturn in the economy, and it might be like Lebanon, or like Yugoslavia, or some of those African countries that have so much diversity. I give this business next door to us less than two years before they break up."

Paul was even more certain of his prediction when he heard that a French man and his wife, recent immigrants, had been added to the staff next door. The French woman would be an office manager who was badly needed. But the French man was another accountant whom Ahrad viewed as a competitor. The French couple insisted on being hired together, or not at all. Ahrad, Abe, and Alfred had a long discussion about that, but they finally hired them; the expanding business actually needed both their skills, and it made hiring very quick and simple.

At first everything seemed to be all right, but soon the trouble started. Francois, the French man, was even faster with arithmetic than Ahrad, but he did it all with such a casual manner that it gave Ahrad his chance to claim that he might be careless. That stirred everyone up. There were a few remarks about how the French might be less meticulous. Ahrad used a magnifying glass to inspect the long columns and formulas the French man fed into the computer, but try as he might, he could find no errors. That never prevented any of them from disliking his casual style.

Then there was the question about how the French woman flounced around the office with her good looks. Stories about French women began to circulate, and Sarah and Millie didn't like that because their husbands did. And even the next generation joined in. Anna and Lester had been to France, and they commented on how independent the French were, all of them. Then Anna and Lester told about how a French taxicab driver had cheated them and how the French people were not very accommodating. So, the printing establishment acted as if there had been a French invasion. Paul Solomon, next door, made repeated observations:

"They got more and more diversity over there," he said to Sadie.

Sadie shook her head knowingly:

"Maybe you're right about that place," she said. "Maybe they're always going to have trouble."

Paul surprised her this time:

"Funny you should say that, because I'm not so sure about my doom and gloom anymore."

Now Sadie was surprised:

"Am I hearing my husband saying I was right?" she asked.

Paul was looking analytical, the way he did when he thought he was on to something new:

"There's som'ting funny happening over there," he said. "They're all of them down on the French couple, and you know what?" He paused to have maximum effect on his wife.

"What, what?" she pushed him.

Paul took on his imperious look, the one he got when he had an answer his wife had never thought about:

"I noticed som'ting," he said. "They're not fighting with each other any more; they're just down on the French couple. For the first time, they've all found som'ting they can agree on. I still say that their business could not have held together longer than two years, the way they were going. But now I think I have to revise my opinion. Now, I think they will stay together as long as they have the French diversity to deal with."

Sadie looked puzzled, so Paul gave her his last words on the whole thing:

"Remember World War II? he asked. "At first the Allies were bosom pals with the Russians. As soon as the Germans were out of the way, the Americans and the Russians were fighting each other. That's how it is with countries, that's how it is with people, and that's how it's gonna be with diversity all over this country. Next door, they'll hold together as long as that French couple is around."

"I think you're saying something crazy," Sadie said.

Paul finished his furniture-bound philosophy:

"People always got troubles with each other, so they got to point the finger at somebody else. It's like anti-Semitism, Sadie. As long as people got a scapegoat, they don't fight each other. As long as I remember, white people were always blaming black people; now black people are blaming whites. You name a group, and I can name some other group that's fightin' them. Right now, next door, all the lightning and thunder is hitting the French couple, so the rest of them will be O.K. That's how people are."

Paul looked very satisfied with himself. He had always wanted to be more than a furniture salesman, and now he pictured himself to be a philosopher. He tacked on his final thought:

"I tell you Sadie, it's not diversity that made America great. It's when diversity takes a back seat and we all think we're the same people that America is great."

Paul noticed that Sadie was speechless and was lowering the corners of her mouth, as if she was considering what he had said. That was about as much as he could hope to get, so he felt more satisfied than ever. He might not have the education and the big words, but he knew he was on to something.

THE GODDESS OF LOVE

A remembrance of his first love in those heady days of high school came to him always, whenever he thought back that far. She had become his goddess of love, and even though he hadn't seen her in years, or perhaps because he had not seen her, the image had grown stronger over the years.

Will Andersen had never deliberately invented a goddess that he could worship. She was just there—she was everything that his mind perceived as the idealized object of his love, and the target of that desire was no longer a real woman.

Now, slightly older, he understood that his first love had never been quite as beautiful as the memory of her. Neither had she been as bright, nor her personality as unique as he had imagined. He knew now that it had not been the girl that was the amazing thing, but the power of desire within himself which had taken hold of him and adorned her beyond all reality.

And yet, despite this knowledge, he could be fooled again. Whenever a new high school girl came along, he thought he had found a new goddess of love. Indeed, he had moved on to another girl, and then another. Finally these all merged together into that goddess of love whom he followed, and all through college he did the same thing again. Each time, the girl looked like that goddess, elevated for admiration—but later, this image of love would gradually fade until she became just what she really was.

Will graduated from college, entered an on-the-job training program in a large corporation, and he was on his way. Time went by rapidly in the scurry of the training program, and some years later he could call himself a corporate executive. Now, he felt that he had, more or less, arrived in this world—not as far as he intended to go, but far enough to feel that he was an established person, a member of the community. He was no longer an interloper student, home for the holidays.

It was at this point that he met Magda. She was warm, sensible, attractive, and occasionally provocative. The forces of that ancient love image came upon Will again. This time it was different because Magda and he were fully grown up, and he had a job, and she was ready for a family. The inevitable happened: he proposed. They were married at her parents' church and bought their first house with a small principal payment, bolstered by generous gifts from their parents.

After eight months in the new house, with the love-image gone, they began to look at each other, seeing the real thing for the first time. What they saw was only partially satisfactory. But here they took different paths. Magda accepted the new reality as the expected thing, as something she could live with. Her love had staying power, so she could find something deeper in it than just an external appearance to be admired. But Will resented the fading goddess and, without admitting it to himself, began to believe that somewhere out there must be a true incarnation of his love-image. He did love Magda, but his love took on that strange form which makes a man believe that he can love someone else at the same time.

They were honest enough to face each other in their new situation, and since they had taken psychology courses in college, they knew that they should talk about it.

Will started it:

"They taught us that if you talk everything out, it will be much better."

She answered curtly:

"They taught us the same thing—I guess it's pretty standard stuff."

Will interrupted before she could say more:

"I guess we like each other—it's just that there's no magic."

"Are you saying I've lost my magic?" she asked in that feminine tone that sends a warning signal.

"No, no," he asserted quickly, "I mean that we both recognize the same thing."

"O.K.," she said, "but I'm beginning to think that talking things out works better in the classroom than it does here."

"Maybe it's like this for everybody," he quickly threw in, hoping to patch things a little.

"Maybe," she responded, "but I've heard some of my friends say that their marriage is just marvelous. 'Course, it's hard to tell if they're honest about it."

He persisted with information from the psychology course in which he had earned a B minus grade:

"My psychology professor said that if you keep talking, it serves like a treatment; he called it ventilation therapy."

"Yeah, yeah," she said, "but I get the feeling that ventilation blows a lot of air around without really making anything look brighter."

"Maybe we need a therapist," he ventured.

"I can't stand those people," she said.

The discussion was over for the time being. Gradually life settled into the humdrum of their jobs, occasional weekend trips, some dining out, a rare movie, and lots of television. Eventually, Magda got pregnant, and they became the parents of a lovely little girl. They called her Bonny. As far as their marriage bond was concerned, nothing seemed to get worse, and nothing got better—it just went along. For five years it went along, and perhaps it would always have been like that, except that a new employee showed up at Will's office. It was a woman.

Rachel was a new office manager who immediately lived up to her job description. She had a figure which could easily compete with the figures on the graphs of the investments made by the corporation, and many men in the firm believed that she was even more efficient than she was. Will could see her clearly at first, but then that old illusion, that image of a goddess to worship, began to surface again. He spent more and more time looking at Rachel, more and more time thinking about her. Eventually he began to take her out to dinner, but he felt guilty all the time. They talked about business, and she began by describing new methods of personnel management. They were really old methods. But like most personnel managers, she introduced old methods with a few new wrinkles and felt that she had made a breakthrough. She described it this way:

"We try to make each employee feel that she, or he, is a part of management."

Will was watching her full lips forming the words, as she continued:

"One can get much more out of people that way," she said, while he saw her breathing a little faster in her animation over the subject. He joined in:

"This personnel business really interests you, doesn't it? Me, I'm more interested in making predictions based upon those graphs of stocks and bonds." As he said this, he was really thinking more about her curves than those in financial data sheets.

Rachel was the new kind of career woman. She was attractive in a very polished kind of way—not a hair out of place and her makeup boldly applied. She wore a neat business jacket on top, with a skirt barely long enough to extend below the coat. Her clipped speech, combined with her appearance, were meant to convey a sense of extreme efficiency, whether it was there or not.

The love-image, the grand illusion, grew faster and faster in Will's mind, and of course he could no longer see that she was really quite an ordinary person of moderately good looks and average ability. He was enthralled, and since she was still out of his reach, Rachel could be seen as that paragon of love that he always searched for. She therefore appeared to be much more attractive than his wife. Rachel knew how to reinforce that image by casually confiding to Will that she had no interest in marriage, but sex was to be enjoyed. She made it a habit to slip this information out to a man when she wanted to set him on fire.

Magda had only seen Rachel once or twice when she picked up her husband at work. But she knew all about it—some people would have called it woman's intuition. Magda could see in one glance the slick look on Rachel's face and body; it was the look that men fall for, even though the appearance is as common as computer monitors in every office building. Magda also noticed that Will often described office activities by starting the sentence with Rachel's name, or something Rachel said or did. Besides that, Magda realized that she was getting less personal attention from her husband. So, intuition really had nothing to do with it; it was just the sum of many casual observations. Magda's perception was keen, and her alarm mechanisms were on high alert. She knew all about love-images and goddesses in her husband's eyes.

But poor Magda didn't know what to do, or which way to turn. She was not a fighting type, so she watched helplessly, as if she were having a bad dream about sitting on a beach unable to move while the tide was rising.

Meanwhile, Will was careening out of control in the office. He did still love Magda, but the new love was relentless in its power. How could any wife compete with the image of idealized beauty which engulfed Will at every turn? The new relationship became obvious to Horace, Will's closest friend in the office. Horace had grown up with Will in high school and knew him very well. He wouldn't have butted in, but one day Will praised Rachel openly:

"That new office manager named Rachel is the best addition to this office. She's quite a knockout too."

Horace wanted to appear casual about it:

"She seems O.K.," he said.

Will went on describing her attributes, and Horace was looking more and more puzzled—they weren't seeing the same thing.

Horace took the right tack:

"You know," he said, "you're acting entirely different in the office, and if you keep that up, you could threaten your job. Remember that the boss is very conservative and doesn't like disruptions in the office. If he finds out about you and Rachel and takes it into his head that it's bad for the company image, he might even fire you."

The thought that he might actually get fired made Will somewhat more sober than he had been in the past when seized by his love-image. At least, it made Will continue to talk with Horace, who was fortunately better at listening than gossiping. Horace was a good choice for other reasons: he had a broader education than his work required; he was well-read; and he was thoughtful. He listened to the whole story and Will's admission of an upcoming adventure, and he searched for the best way to reach his friend:

"Do you remember your many love affairs before marriage? Each time you told me about a new goddess of love, you were sure this was the real one, and each time they dwindled into nothing. Doesn't that tell you something?"

"I know what you're saying," answered Will, "but this sure feels right."

"That's the point. That's the very point," Horace said intensely. "You're only talking about feelings, not sense. And your history of feelings like these have all been short-lived."

Horace went on to put out a theory to go along with his advice, and he waxed a bit philosophical:

"I have a theory about the way people form these crazy love-images that have nothing to do with reality. I think it's nature's way of making sure that the race survives. If ancient people had not been seized by these impulses, had not lost all judgement periodically, they might not have made enough children for the race to survive—it was a necessary trait for successful evolution. But that doesn't mean that it's the sensible thing to act on now."

Will hated it whenever Horace went into his theoretical approach. But his friend had just told him what a fool he was, without saying it outright. And the reminder about his school passions which flared and faded sounded true enough. But even with that memory, he couldn't believe it applied to him right now, and he said so.

Horace could see that Will was beyond reach, so he took another approach:

"O.K., O.K.," he said, "but do me a great favor. Instead of doing something rash, just put it all off for one year, say until January. Spend time with your hobby, with your gun collection."

Putting off a goddess was not part of the normal response to passion for Will. He nodded his head in agreement, but Rachel stayed on his mind, and his behavior was unchanged.

The action in the office was nothing compared to his wife's inner turmoil at home. Magda was alone all the time, and that sparked her jealousy and hatred. The feeling of helplessness made Magda desperate. She decided that Will had gone off the deep end, but she also decided that he must remain her husband—that he was the man who belonged to her, not to that other woman. Magda felt violated, but she was determined that Rachel would not get her man. Events had unleashed forces beyond her control—she was completely changed, like a woman obsessed. She clenched her teeth and laid out her plans.

It all came to a head one day when she was in the family room, and her desperate eye rested on the gun collection that Will had in a glass case. She knew that there was a little box of shiny bullets in the drawer of the cabinet. Without thinking it through, she opened the drawer and the glass case. She stood looking down at one small handgun. Magda was crying now as her fingers slid over the cold shiny metal in the padded box. She didn't quite pick it up; she just slid her hand over it as the tears fell down her cheeks. Finally, she closed the case and the drawer, but it wasn't over.

During this very moment, back in their office building, Will and Rachel were blithely talking again without the slightest idea that jealousy could transform a gentle wife who loved too much into a figure who might threaten their lives. There they were acting like usual, while elsewhere a decision was being made within a brain now deeply disturbed. Still, until now, Magda had always been a rational woman. Violence was on her mind, but she couldn't quite decide; she couldn't quite move on it, and the days went by.

At the office, Will couldn't quite decide to leave his wife, but he wouldn't give up Rachel, and he couldn't bring himself to run away with her. He reached a state of protracted and painful indecision.

In the midst of all this, Horace was suddenly transferred to an office in Chicago, so Will's prop was gone.

Days went by, then weeks. Will and Magda hung on this way with Will unable to make a move and still coming home to Magda at night. He decided that he loved them both, but that was hardly a decision worth making.

Meantime Rachel was growing impatient and showing it, despite all her original protestations that she was uninterested in marriage. The impatience made the goddess image lose some of its sheen. But still, the unpossessed Rachel hung there in front of Will like bait that can't be reached without pain.

At home, Magda was also hanging in midair, in a murderous mood. She wanted things settled, but her hand was held back when she realized that things were not quite moving Rachel's way either. Magda began to vacillate in a curious way. Some days she would convince herself that if her husband had not left her so far, he never would. On other days, like after a probing question from a friend, she would come home and stand in the family room again, opening the gun case and letting her fingers slide over that cold metal.

It was all very tense and threatening, and it dragged and dragged. One year later, they were still hanging on without quite moving on. Then something happened. It was only a message that came in a letter to Will, but the impact was like a hammer blow!

The morning mail had brought a letter from Horace in Chicago, and on the white pages, Will read words that he could not believe. Good old Horace, wise old Horace, had apparently gone off the deep end. He was separated from his wife, and he had taken up with a much younger woman. After only four months with her, he couldn't stand her, so he tried to go back to his wife, but she wouldn't let him in. Horace was living in a rented room and eating at the local diner. That was too much for Will. Nothing else could have reached him so powerfully, could have opened his eyes. His trusted friend, his most dependable friend, the wise one in whom he had so much confidence, had apparently flipped.

And then he thought about Horace's words, about the love goddess that grasps a man once in a while, and how within her grip a man loses control. Will started muttering to himself:

"God," he said, "if it can happen to Horace, it can happen to anybody."

He knew that he would have to write to Horace's wife, who was a wonderful person and a good friend. Will didn't know how he would write the letter, but it had to be done.

A while later, he was still muttering to himself:

"That dumbbell," he said.

Later that afternoon, Will bought a box of chocolates and a dozen roses. He had them delivered to Magda who was so surprised that she let herself sink into an easy chair, clutching the roses in one hand and the chocolates in the other. For a moment, she couldn't think of anything else. Then, she began to form an image in her mind of a goddess laid to rest, and it made her smile. She even harbored an expectation of her own, that perhaps she herself would be the last goddess after all.

A BOWL OF SOUP

Those college days hovered about in their memories like full glasses of wine to be drained at will—and refilled once again. John Sitwell, Robert Shaw, and Albert Denver had been close friends in college, and the remembrance of college days, full of idle times and pleasure, was a never-ending source of entertainment. But a few years after graduation, success or disaster were waiting for them, and each would cast his lot merely by the unseasoned choices he made, or failed to make.

It was Robert, with his blond hair and blue eyes, who first broke the old college pattern and told Albert about it.

"I'm getting married," he announced firmly to his friend.

Albert paused and then responded:

"So you're really going to do it?" he asked.

"Sure am," said Robert. "I've got a good job and a nice apartment, and I've picked the girl I want—you know Christine. No point in putting it off."

Albert knew all about Robert's conventional upper-class family. His parents were always busy during the week, attended church on Sundays, and divided the rest of their time between sports and travel. They owned a fancy house in the suburbs, and they belonged to local clubs. Robert Shaw reflected all that; he had accepted it all as the norm, and one could see it in the way he dressed, the way he spoke, and in his clear definition of his own future. Albert seemed to question it all:

"You really want to settle in just like that?" he asked.

Robert nailed it down again:

"No sense in delaying it," he said. "May as well get an early start."

Since Robert Shaw was launching into a standard way of life, with a conventional way of making a living and a conventional family plan, it was a relatively uncomplicated project, at least for now.

Robert Shaw accepted tradition as the only way to go because it was the path of least resistance, and because it would lead to early security. But Robert, under his handsome outside features, was a complex man with many desires. He dressed in a business suit because it led to early acceptance, but in other moods, he nursed a desire to throw it all off and find a more daring facade. He was getting married because it established him in the community, but he harbored desires for other excitement. He attended concerts and lectures because they gave him class, but he yearned for more lively entertainment. And most of all, he climbed rapidly into the business world of public relations and advertising. He was good at it and made money, but he had always imagined himself a greater person who would contribute something on the world stage or in a public arena such as politics. So he set out on a simple path, but he concealed a powerful desire to accomplish something for which the world would remember him.

Albert was in a different world. He kept wearing his jeans and avoided any serious choices, but of course when he continued on his college student pattern, choices were made for him, and some doors were closed merely by his standing still in an old pattern. He did get a simple sales job and acquired a steady girlfriend who drifted into his life. He even thought he loved her, but he wasn't sure. He never faced the issue as a question since he planned to flow into conjugal life without commitment. Jeanette was willing to live with him, and no hard commitments were necessary, or even desired. So they moved into the same apartment, shared a bed, and lived as man and wife without the encumbrances of full legal commitment. They often congratulated themselves upon their way of life:

"This is the only way to live," Albert would say to Jeanette, and she concurred:

"The marriage vows are unnecessary," she would say, "and that piece of paper is no more meaningful than our promises to each other."

Without fanfare, without a church, without family approvals, and without clergy, they had defined their own meaningful relationship. There was not the slightest doubt in their minds about the superiority and lack of hypocrisy in this arrangement. They reveled in what they considered a slightly rebellious attitude toward society. Albert and Jeanette would have enjoyed their conjugal love somewhat less if they had understood how little the modern conventional world was concerned with what they did, or did not do.

John Sitwell was another matter altogether. He watched Albert's ways and Robert's simple path with a mixture of amazement and disdain. He remembered the college days when they had taken part in student demands and student government activism. And now, only a few years later, Robert Shaw was always dressed in a business suit and fitting in, while Albert kept the blue jeans and the loose way of life, but seemed to have forgotten all about the lofty ideas for making a better world.

John Sitwell was determined to find a better way, so he kept his long black hair in a pony tail, and he decided that life in a commune was the answer. There he could form bonds of love with brethren and sisters, bonds that extended beyond a selfish tie to a single partner. He knew which commune to go to because he had met a woman in a bar who told him all about the Roscoe Community. The commune was located in the country in an isolated stretch of Montana. The members welcomed anyone who would share in their beliefs and in their daily chores, yet each one was free to live a private life when he or she was away from the commune. Elaine, the girl at the bar, explained:

"Here I am," she said, "in a bar in New York just because I felt like coming on a vacation. No one at the Roscoe Community would object to that. It's the way we set up the commune, and that's the way it runs. The trouble with other community groups is that they restrict the lives of their members too much."

John agreed heartily. Only a month later, he took the $3850 dollars he had saved and headed for Montana. A plane took him to the nearest town, a bus carried him to the nearest highway, and then he walked the rest of the way, following the directions given to him by his bar friend, Elaine.

Upon arrival, he found a small development with one real house and many smaller improvised buildings, each with a wood stove for the winter. The real house was a big old farmhouse which the commune used for meetings and administration.

John found Elaine soon after arrival, and she welcomed him with open arms, taking him around to meet all the other members of the Roscoe Commune—there were forty-five adults and an unidentified number of children. The current head of the commune sat in a makeshift office in the main building. He explained to John that each person was either taken in to one of the shacks or could build his own. When the Montana winter got too bad, they would all pack into the main house for as long as it was necessary

"A lot of the year you can stay in the unit you are assigned to, since each one has a little wood stove," he said, almost reassuringly. As soon as the head man had spoken, Elaine announced that John would be welcome to stay in her unit because she had already spoken to the others.

They walked over to carry his belongings into the shack and meet the other people in that unit. The building was supported by two-by-fours, mounted on five-by-five beams of pressure-treated wood; there was no excavation, but the floor was poured cement on which several old rugs had been laid. There were four small bedrooms opening on a central living quarter which had an area for cooking. A small bathroom seemed to function by means of a chemical tank. John was immediately introduced to another young man and two women with a collection of five children who seemed to belong to everybody. The young man had a stern face, but evidently did not oppose John's arrival. The two women had smiles on their faces, the kind of smiles that are necessary for new arrivals.

The house was not dirty, but it wasn't clean. The children's clothes were not disreputable, but they weren't neat. All the possessions, including extra clothes, were strewn around, although it was evident that Elaine had been picking up. She explained how well they lived:

"We all share everything we've got, and we all take part in the chores. It's not every man for himself as it is in the outside world. You never have to get a baby sitter because one of us is always around, and the children get along pretty well because they've grown up this way." At that moment, one of the children was tearing a little truck away from a smaller child.

John felt a need to establish his life philosophy with the other inhabitants, so he spoke loudly enough for all of them to hear:

"Caring about each other is pretty much what I'm looking for," he said with some uncertainty. He meant it, but he was afraid it didn't come across strongly enough. However one of the women spoke up right away:

"Oh, yeah," she said, "we care about each other."

"We all pool our money together just like everything else," said the young man with the stern face.

John tried to look casual, but he hadn't realized before this moment that his meager savings had just been appropriated. He tried to make the best of it. You could look upon it as an investment, he thought, but like most people on Wall Street, he wasn't sure if it was a safe investment, or what the returns would be.

Elaine pointed to one of the bedrooms and said, "You can put your bag and your bedroll in there where I stay, if you want to, but we settle down pretty much wherever we feel like."

There was an expectant expression on the faces of the other two women as they assessed in a fraction of a second how things were going to shake out. John hesitated. Then, without saying anything, he just put his bag down in the room Elaine had pointed to. She smiled.

The whole commune approach had all started slowly for John. Everything had remained in his control as long as he was just making plans to come to Montana, but after arrival it all went very fast. He was suddenly standing there in a room with four other adults, and the others were clearly measuring him to see whether he would fit in. It was not the kind of social climate in which he could just say, "I don't think I'm ready to move in with Elaine." Nor could he say, "I really don't want to pool all our funds."

As Elaine followed him into the bedroom, she clarified their relationship a little:

"Just because we're in the same room, doesn't mean we have to sleep in the same bed," she said. "Each person decides what he wants to do about that for himself." That might have satisfied John, but actually he was more concerned about the money question.

In the months that followed, John did sort of take up with Elaine. She was good-looking, casual and outgoing, and she had a palpably sensual approach to men that welcomed them without apparent encumbrance. People in the commune shifted partners at times, so there seemed to be no hard commitment, even though jealousies and possessiveness were no less than in the outside world.

In time, John Sitwell realized that nothing that he had done in college had ever controlled his life as permanently as the commune. After all, in college there was a day of graduation, an end point. But here in the commune there was no graduation day, so you either stayed, or you had to make a break for it.

So there it was! Three friends, John Sitwell, Albert Denver, and Robert Shaw had each found a different way of life, each casting his lot in a radically different path.

One year and a half later, Albert told Robert a sobering story about their absent friend, John Sitwell:

"He sent me a long letter," Albert began, "about what it's like to live in a commune. I think he's going to give it up and come home."

"No kidding?" said Robert, with feigned surprise and some satisfaction that his opinion about communes would be vindicated. "What happened?"

"The letter was long," Albert repeated. "The trouble was that everybody in the place wanted to be the leader; the time spent on chores precluded doing much of anything else; the shacks were cold; and when they moved to the main house, it was packed with bodies. Besides that, the money ran short; the rotation of cooks made some meals good and others terrible; the children were underfoot all the time, even for a single guy; the pets were not cared for; the house-cleaning teams often left the place a shambles; the neighbors were hostile; and John missed not having possessions and a place he could call his own. Finally, any love he had for Elaine sort of evaporated when she brought two more men into the commune. Other than that, he said it was great."

Robert Shaw began to laugh, but Albert stopped him:

"I wouldn't laugh at him. I think we could all use the things that those places promise—the idea of all working for the common good. It was just that John couldn't make it work, and the others couldn't either."

Shaw was not impressed and he interrupted:

"Isn't that the point? It's all nice sentiment, but it never works and never has for any length of time anywhere. What strikes me about these commune people is that they nourish this love for everybody idea so fervently that they don't have enough love left over to give to any one person. There's another thing: I think most of them join a commune mostly to escape the world they know, rather than because they have any clear idea of what to create in their new one."

"I know," said Albert, "but you have to give them credit for trying. I think John is like that; he wants a better world, but he hasn't found it. 'Course I'm not too sure I've found it either."

Albert was more sympathetic than Robert Shaw to John Sitwell's plight. Albert and his girlfriend Jeanette still wore jeans all the time, almost like uniforms. But Albert didn't like the idea of group living. He and Jeanette still congratulated themselves all the time on living together without marriage and without a commune.

Of course, the stresses of living together were the same for them as they are for married people. So the usual fights developed—there were disagreements on finances; they had rather divergent interests; and she wanted a child, while he did not. He also used his credit card very freely, while Jeanette worked hard to save every penny every month.

They made every effort to adjust their differences, and they were experts at presenting their long philosophical discussions with all the high moral tone of the 1960's. But there were needs that would not go away and defied philosophy. One was put forth by Jeanette:

"I guess a man doesn't feel the need to have a child the way I do. For me, life is not complete. Can you understand that?"

"Sure" said Albert easily, without any real insight. He never saw that his lack of interest in a child was perceived by her as a lack of commitment. So the issue sat there, like a small thorn under the skin that you are unable to pick out with a needle. It was not a sudden violent pain, but it was always there and always sore.

On top of that, there was the question of money:

"Have you got any idea what it's like for me," she would ask, "to work all day just like you, come home with my paycheck, and then find out that you've already spent it?"

"We don't have to pay the credit charge for a while," he would answer weakly.

That made Jeanette's face turn red with anger:

"That's the worst part of it," she finally screamed. "You have this notion that an extra charge on the credit card is not as bad as getting out your wallet and your dollar bills."

"I know that," he would say in defense. And then she would respond sharply:

"You know, and you don't know; you know, but you still do it."

The childless state, with less and less money, could not last. Eventually, exasperated, they decided to part company. And once again, they congratulated themselves on not having gotten married because they could just walk out without any trouble. Or could they? That was the part neither of them had understood.

Soon they squabbled about who would keep the apartment, who owed what on back rent, who owned the rugs, the draperies, the luggage, the furniture, and all the bric-a-brac. They ended up in court, and each one had to have a lawyer who pointed out the difficulties of sorting things out without a marriage contract. Albert protested:

"There are plenty of troubles sorting things out between married people too," he said.

"Yes," agreed his lawyer, "I've got to grant you that. But a marriage contract is more clearly defined by the law, so it's easier to sort out." The fight went on a long time, the legal costs kept growing, and now at last Albert understood what that marriage paper was all about.

By now, John Sitwell was back in his home town with a job at the local hardware store and a rented room to live in until he got his feet on the ground. He was starting over.

People in town who watched the three former college friends could see that two of them, Albert Denver and John Sitwell, had never gotten very far. The only thing that saved them was that they didn't demand very much. On the other hand, Robert Shaw was a real success story with even greater expectations. No one would deny that.

Robert Shaw acted fully satisfied, and a little smug, about his life choices. He even gave his two friends advice, and his wife Christine gave them even more advice. But under all this, there was something brewing. Robert still wanted fame, and he wanted it without flexibility, without compromise—he had to have it.

One day Albert and John noticed something odd about Robert. He kept trying new hobbies, new entertainment, and trips all over the place, with or without Christine. He drank quite a bit. Whatever was sneaking up on Robert was subtle, but virulent. At times he wasn't properly shaved, and his clothes were no longer freshly pressed. Sometimes he looked sleepy in the middle of the day.

Albert and John ignored it all until the night when they decided to make a surprise visit at Robert's house. They came up the walk and rang the bell, but there was no answer. They waited a while, and then one of them pushed a little on the door until it opened. They called, but there was no answer, so they decided they must check the place out. Robert's family was apparently out, but Robert was there. They found him in the living room lying on a couch, too drunk to talk, his hair rumpled, his shirt out of his pants, and one shoe on the floor. It was the saddest sight they had ever seen.

For a couple of hours they worked with him and fed him coffee. After a long time, he began to talk, even though his speech was slurred:

"I feel kind of funny about this," he began, "but I do have a problem, and you two guys are my best friends."

It was strange for John and Albert to see their successful friend like that. In his life, he had done the right thing at every turn. He had a full marriage, two children, a fancy house, a good career, and golf on Tuesdays at the country club. What more could he want?

He started to mumble something about wanting more, wanting some kind of meaning in his life. He couldn't express it well this night, but a couple of months later when he was sober, he could say it better. He harped back to the college days:

"We were really going to set things right in the world," he told them, "and somehow we never did."

"Your way of life sounds pretty good to me now," admitted John, looking at it from his new perspective.

"Yeah," answered Robert, "it looks good, but its not complete. It's not finished; it's not anything that amounts to much. It's just a kind of a shallow suburban routine. And there's another thing: the nuclear family, which I thought had everything, has its limitations too, but I don't know what's missing."

John tried to produce an answer:

"The nuclear family, by its very definition, is a little group made up of a man and a woman and their children. They look out for themselves and don't care very deeply about looking out for anybody else."

Robert would have argued that point in the old days, but now he knew that there was something to it, so he just asked a question:

"So what's the answer?"

None of them could produce that, so they sat around talking about it for a while, and then they went home. Each time they met, they would talk about it again. There was never an answer, so they just went on living as best they could. The world wasn't great, but there was no place else to go.

Eventually, John Sitwell married a girl from Idaho; Albert found a real wife with whom he was more reasonable because he expected less than the first time; and Robert stuck it out with Christine.

When, from time to time, the three college friends met in the local diner and talked about how life had turned out, none of them was fully satisfied, but only one was in turmoil. Robert tried to say it without showing the agitation that he could not shake off:

"When I got married and earned a lot of money, I thought you guys were off on a bat with your communes and your meaningful relationships, but it's hard for anyone to make life mean very much, isn't it?"

None of them could produce any new ideas, so they just sat. Robert felt it more than the other two because he couldn't let go. He couldn't give up the great shiny future and the fame he never got.

When they broke up, Robert walked along the darkening streets heading for home. But suddenly he remembered that his two friends had told him they were going to try something new; they were going to the local soup kitchen to volunteer their time helping out. When they had spoken about it, Robert hadn't thought about it much. But now that he was wandering alone down a dark and lonely street, he was seized by a sudden desperation to do something different. He turned in his tracks and headed for the hall where the food was offered to the poor. When he arrived at the soup kitchen, his two friends were amazed to see him, but they put him to work. The three friends stood side by side, handing out the food to the indigent people who lined up on the other side of the table.

John Sitwell was the first to see something special. An old man in ragged clothes appeared in front of him. The man's face was drawn and thin, but he tried to look pleasant. When John handed him a bowl of hot soup, the man's face lit up, and he grasped the bowl eagerly with both hands.

As the homeless men and women moved along, Albert Denver was the next one to see something special in the eyes of a thin young woman as he handed her a bowl of soup. It wasn't much of an expression; it was just that her eyes were fixed on that bowl of soup. Albert knew instantly that he held the essential of life, the only thing that counted, and he was passing it on to her.

Robert worked hard handing out the food, moving the people along, starting to organize the volunteers. It was like another business venture for him, an activity that had to be accomplished efficiently. At the end of the evening, John and Albert promised to come again. Robert told the people at the kitchen that he would let them know if he could find the time again.

Months went by as each man moved on with his life. Nothing seemed to change until a dreadful rainy night when John got the call from Christine Shaw's sister:

"I'm calling for Christine," she said, "because she can't come to the phone. I'm afraid I have very bad news, and Christine told me to call you and another one of Robert's friends named Albert Denver."

"Oh sure," said John, "Albert and I have been good friends of Robert's since college. Hope he and Christine are O.K."

The sister spoke mechanically:

"I'm afraid it's about as bad as it can get. Can you come down to the house?"

John made a rush call to Albert, and they made their way down to the Shaw's house. They were puzzled since neither of them knew what was going on. They knew that Robert drank too much, so they wondered if the bad news had something to do with that.

The Shaw house was a mansion. There were several cars in the circular drive and an ambulance with flashing lights.

"Good God," said John, "one of them must be sick."

They hurried into the house, but the police stopped them in the hall. There was the usual hubbub that's always around when disaster strikes. The information came in little bits, as if no one was sure how much to tell these two friends. Eventually it all came out.

Robert was dead! He was lying there in his business suit on the couch where he had been found. He was surrounded by alcohol and drugs, and he had apparently taken too much of both, probably on purpose. There wasn't much else that John and Albert could learn, so they made the usual effort to console Robert's wife and ask if there was anything they could do.

After that day, there were only two friends who met periodically at the diner for their informal reunions. John Sitwell and Albert Denver had never fully figured out what life was all about, but each of them had made an adjustment—they were able to live it out.

"I never figured out what it was about Robert," Albert said to John. "He seemed to have it all, but he couldn't find any meaning to life."

John thought a while, and then he asked a question:

"Do you remember the night he came to help at the soup kitchen? It was a special night for me. I didn't know what life was all about until that night, but when I saw the face of an old man as I handed him a bowl of soup, I knew that I held it all in my hands."

Albert remained skeptical:

"I can't see how a bowl of soup could make the difference."

John still looked as if he had the answer:

"It wasn't just the soup," he mused, "It was more the old man's eyes. He had given up on all the other troubles that plague us from day to day, and he was reaching for the only thing that really mattered. So I learned from him. Robert stood there right next to me, but he never saw any of that—he never read their eyes, but looked only into his own, even when he handed them a bowl of soup."

THE INNKEEPER

Casimir was born in Katovice, in Poland, where he enjoyed kindergarten. His young father was a rising star in the heavy machinery works that were made possible by the iron and coal mining which surrounded the city. His mother reflected the cultural wealth of Katovice and its ties to nearby Krakow. It was easy to predict that Casimir would flourish in this productive town and in the love of his family, but of course, none of these predictions took Germany into account. That large neighbor was thrashing about destroying its inadequate Weimar Republic and changing it into something worse. But Casimir knew nothing about that. Nor did Casimir know anything about Franz Mueller who lived in a small town in Eastern Prussia. No one, by any stretch of the imagination, would have suggested that little Casimir in Katovice would one day have a catastrophic meeting with Franz Mueller from Prussia.

Mueller was a school teacher, but during his own early days as a student, he had always been described by his instructors as unremarkable. That condescending word had stuck in his memory and came to him repeatedly as a bitter recollection since he wanted to amount to something great. After graduation he applied to a university and tried to obtain a position as instructor, but he was rejected. Despite this rocky academic start and because of his persistence, he was able to became a school teacher. He eventually liked his position because the classroom furnished him a place where, surrounded by twenty-five students, he was the sole authority, the only remarkable person in the room. In that limited setting, he knew more than anyone else, and he gave orders that had to be observed. Yes, the Prussian town still harbored a comfortable feeling for a teacher whose authority could not be challenged.

One day, Franz Mueller was walking through the town square when he saw a crowd listening to an animated speaker in uniform. In back of the speaker was a large sign with an inscription, "National Socialist Party." The man was yelling:

"The New Order has come to Germany. Every German will be a part of it, every town will be a part of it, and one day the whole world will be brought under this flag."

He pointed to one of his banners as he continued:

"A superior race will lead the world, and that race is the German people."

The audience cheered for itself, and Franz Mueller did not laugh. He took it all very seriously. Here was a stirring martial air with a philosophy that he could relate to, and he felt strangely exhilarated.

As National Socialism gained power in Germany, Mueller felt pride in the new party chairman, the one who, like himself, had not done well in school. That son of Alois Hitler had dropped out of high school and twice failed the examination for the academy of arts. But he had charisma in abundance and magnetic oratory, and he practiced ruthless suppression of opposition which allowed him to rise to power. Mueller followed the career of this rising star with fascination and could imagine a parallel in himself. Soon, Hitler had a more direct effect upon Mueller. The National Socialist Party subverted liberal education in schools—instead the Party wanted teachers to emphasize political expressions of power for the Third Reich. This fit in well with Mueller's views and gained him favorable attention with the local militia.

When Mueller was called for military service, he went willingly. With the rapid military expansion of the coming war, he was able to gain a commission as a Leutnant and later a promotion to Kapitan. It was a set of promotions for Mueller that he would never before have dreamed possible in the rigid hierarchy of Prussian militarism. While military service felt like a demotion to other teachers and professors, it felt like a promotion to Franz Mueller.

In combat, Mueller comported himself with considerable courage. He was respected by the men under his command, especially during the crushing of Poland's resistance with its courageous, but ill-prepared, cavalry still riding horses. In the later years of the war, Mueller was assigned to control a small Polish town and a prison camp. Away from the larger death camps, this prison was no less evil because its isolation permitted anonymous acts of tyranny. Commander Mueller's rapid rise to power allowed his more sinister side to mushroom into a frightful force.

Mueller's handsome chiseled face fit admirably under the military hat. He had adopted a powerful military bearing whose Aryan appearance was the ideal of German culture. Once the Polish invasion was over and before the tougher days to come, Mueller was at the height of his imperious growth. He underwent a progressive transfiguration, born of his former frustration, and he suddenly released his malice upon the victims who lay within his grasp. A sympathetic observer would have said that he suddenly became unraveled, but a more perceptive witness would have said that rage and sadism had always been inside him—that it was merely the situation that allowed it to burst forth. When Franz Mueller found men, women, and children fully under his control, it released the depravity of which he was capable. He understood only too well that his superiors in nearby towns and in Berlin would hold him accountable for the efficiency with which he ran the camp, but would be more likely to praise him than to punish him for ruthlessness. At first his commands were merely harsh and were carried out by men under his command in the guise of maintaining discipline. But in time, he ceased to search for excuses to perform acts of barbarism and cowardice. There were even stories among the German soldiers that the Commandant personally entered the cells of prisoners at night to rape and torture his victims. Mueller had a clean-cut external military bearing and a savage interior!

The prisoners referred to Mueller as "The Savage," a name that was not merely derisive, but depicted what they saw, what they knew him to be. There was no longer anything about Franz Mueller that would have allowed any of his former pupils, or their parents, to recognize him. And the men under his command split into groups—those who eagerly participated in his shameful acts and those who disapproved but never risked opposition. And when out of earshot, even they called him "The Savage."

Until late in the war, little Casimir in Katovice had miraculously been spared the worst of the war. But a day came when his father was arrested because of his prominence in industry and because of his courageous opposition to the occupation forces. The soldiers who came for his father also took Casimir's mother and the ten-year-old Casimir, perhaps as pawns with which to force his father to cooperate with production of war machinery for the Third Reich. The little family was placed in a cell in a prison whose recently promoted Commandant was named Mueller.

The hour was coming closer when the Commandant Mueller would meet little Casimir. The fateful night came when the Commandant entered into the cell of a young family that remained proud and defiant. Mueller knew how to deal with resistance. He threatened the wife and the child, which usually worked. But when the young father refused to return to his factory to lead Polish workers in the manufacture of heavy machinery for the production of weapons to be used against the Allies, Mueller made an assessment. He would not waste time with open resistance, and he gave a simple command to his soldiers. He pointed to the young father and said:

"Take this man out into the courtyard, and if he does not cooperate by the time he gets there, shoot him."

The young mother began to beg:

"Please, please, don't do this," she said. "He resists only because he loves Poland, and he will not be a part of creating weapons to kill the Allies. You must understand that. It's not because he wants to resist your commands."

Mueller was beginning to feel the sense of power that he enjoyed. The woman was becoming submissive. But when the shot rang out in the courtyard, her skin turned ashen gray, she clenched her jaws, and her face became proud and defiant. This was what Mueller could not stand. His rage was without control as his face turned red with anger. He began to beat her, and when she resisted, he beat her until she lost consciousness.

Crouching in a corner was their ten-year-old son, Casimir. Forced to watch, tears streamed down his face. The eyes of the child reflected the stages of brutality. At first there was disbelief, then anxiety, and finally the terror which was supplanted by a blank expression as his eyes glazed, unable to look. The end came when his mother ceased to breathe.

Mueller felt no sense of guilt. Maintaining his lofty attitude, he placed the blame for violence directly upon the victims. If only these people had cooperated, there might never be a need for these scenes. He remained oblivious to his own sadism. He barely glanced at the boy in the corner, but Casimir's eyes were now fixed upon the face of his parents' executioner. Fear and hatred were mixed in the indelible mark that was forming in his brain. In a strange kind of way, he could not remove his eyes from the face of the Commandant. The effect was like a hot iron that left its permanent mark.

Casimir survived the moment only because he was ignored and thrown in with other children who became nameless. And when liberation came, he was moved from hand to hand, from school to school, from town to town, until he finished his primary education. Then he moved out to work. Casimir became one of thousands of displaced people in Poland, but like most of them, he gradually pieced together a new life and became an errand boy in a store. As the years went by, Casimir's native intelligence and maturity allowed him to work his way up, and eventually he became an office manager. He was seemingly assimilated into the post-war community, but there was one indelible image in his mind that would not assimilate—it was the face of the man who had torn his family away.

Night after night in his dreams and when he awakened, he would see the face of Franz Mueller, as if he were still there looming over him. Casimir often spoke with his friend Wladislaw:

"I shall find that man one day, if he is still alive," he would say. Wladislaw had seen enough of the terror himself to under-stand the feeling, but he knew the obsession might destroy his friend:

"Think of other things, Casimir, as much as you can," he would say lamely.

Casimir never answered, but his eyes remained fixed upon the target. Whenever he was at home, he would search copies of documents which might help locate the infamous cause of his memories. Casimir contacted a number of groups which searched for war criminals, and he examined lists of prison commandants, but the name of der Kapitan Franz Mueller failed to appear among survivors. Wladislaw kept trying to coax his friend to give up his obsession and compulsion to search. But thoughts of vengeance remained in Casimir because they were as much a part of him as the resiliency that had allowed him to survive, and even thrive. Casimir would never rest.

Years passed without new information, but one day Casimir met an old man who had been in the same prison camp in which his parents died. The man had electrifying news! He knew the name of the town where Franz Mueller had been a school teacher—perhaps, if he were still alive, he had gone back to his home town. Casimir immediately planned his next vacation. By devious means, he was able to obtain a passport to visit East Germany, and he made his way to the former Prussian town where Mueller might be found. At the local school, Casimir inspected every teacher who came and went through the front door. No one looked like Mueller, but Casimir talked with anyone who would listen to him. Finally one Saturday evening, he was in a beer hall and began talking with one of the waitresses. She didn't have the answer, but she had a lead:

"My mother told me about a teacher named Mueller who never came back to this town after the war," she said. "But, perhaps, I can help you find your friend. There is a man who lives in a town about fifty kilometers from here who comes here once or twice a year to drink and sing. He talks a lot about the old school. He's not the man you're looking for because his name is Otto. He's an innkeeper, but he might know other people from the old school."

Casimir drove the fifty kilometers and parked in front of the inn. He entered the dining room and was welcomed by Otto, the genial host and owner. He was a heavyset man, dressed in a Bavarian outfit with short pants. Why he should have dressed that way in a formerly Prussian town was not clear, but Casimir assumed it had something to do with attracting tourists. Otto showed him the dining room and the sitting room, and a desk clerk gave Casimir a key to his room. After cleaning up, Casimir came down for dinner where he had an opportunity to engage Otto in conversation to discover whether he knew anything about former school teachers in nearby towns. Otto tried to be helpful:

"I'm afraid that my business is far-removed from schools and school teachers," he said. "Are you looking for any particular person?"

Casimir wanted a chance to ask a lot of questions anonymously for a while, so he answered vaguely:

"My parents came to this area for one year when my father signed up for technical training. I went to school nearby during that year." Casimir named the town where Mueller had been the teacher, and then he continued:

"There was a boy that I was friendly with named Karl, but I don't know his last name. I also had a teacher who made a great impression on me, but I don't remember his name."

"It's hard to locate anybody without a last name," said the innkeeper, but I'm not surprised that you should not remember last names; that's the way we remember the world when we are children."

Otto shook his head slowly from side to side to show that no particular name came to his memory:

"I'm afraid I'm not very helpful," he said, "but I hope you stay a while, enjoy our hospitality, and perhaps find your friend and your teacher."

After that, Casimir could not think of what to ask, but he knew that Otto regularly visited Mueller's home town. So he kept coming back to the inn hoping that Otto's activities might still lead him to Franz Mueller.

One night, as Casimir sat in the dining room, there was an extraordinary event! It was nothing that anyone else observed—it was just something that happened in Casimir's brain. He was sitting and thinking about his search for Franz Mueller as he casually watched the innkeeper walking back and forth, going about his business. Casimir was looking, without purpose, at the round face of the jolly innkeeper, when he suddenly began to see it differently—as if it were thinner, younger, and more aquiline. Gradually a cold feeling ran down Casimir's neck, prompted by a memory from times past. At first the memory was not clear, but the disagreeable feeling was persistent and became stronger and stronger. Suddenly, as if prompted by that powerful feeling, the new image of the innkeeper's face became sharper in his mind. It was the face of Franz Mueller! All of sudden it came together, and Casimir saw the body of the genial innkeeper with the imagined head of Franz Mueller. It was right. It was real. Casimir could no longer separate the virtual image from the face in front of him.

Casimir was speechless and unable to move. He stared and stared. Yes, it did look like Mueller, but the face and the body were so different. Nonetheless, it had been many years, and Mueller would have aged and perhaps gained weight, causing the face to become rounder. As Casimir searched the face, a gradual sense of fear came over him, and this fear sharpened his remembrance of the terrible day. Suddenly, he could see the event again, and now he thought he could imagine how the face would have changed. Casimir was sweating, and his anger and fear swirled around him until he had to stand up and run from the building.

Once outside, Casimir was able to regain his composure, and he laid out a plan. He would stay for the rest of the week and try to eat in the inn every day. He must be sure, very sure. After returning day after day, Casimir became more and more certain. But now the stark reality made him realized that there must be better proof.

Back home in Poland, Casimir contacted one of the agencies that was tracing war criminals, and he learned all about the evidence that he must collect. The agency sent papers to be filled out, and he was interviewed; then Casimir was advised to go back to his own job—let them handle it, they said, and they would contact him when he was needed to identify or testify.

Months went by, interminably. Casimir called the agency frequently and always got the same answer:

"We are looking into it," the investigator said, "but these things take time. It must be done right, or we will lose, and you will lose."

Six months later, Casimir had a new call from the man in charge of the investigation.

"We've done a careful search, and so far, the evidence is not sufficient. Of course, we never give up, so you should not give up either. If you think of any other evidence, call us back."

Casimir had only one piece of evidence—it was the image of the face in his own mind. Such a memory was sharp in his own brain, but it would be weak in a court of law.

Casimir felt a burning need to remain close to the hated face. Whenever he could take time off, he would ride the train across the border into Germany to visit again the town where Mueller had been a teacher. Then he would hire a car to drive the other fifty kilometers to eat at the inn and to watch. There was no longer any doubt in his mind, but watching was all he could do in spite of the terrible thoughts that came to his mind. He began to make a plan. He would kill the man himself!

When Casimir returned home, he took another step toward his destiny. He bought a revolver, and he stashed it in a drawer of his desk together with a box of shells. Then new thoughts came to mind. Would he confront the man? Or would he just walk up behind him, fire, and run? Once again the question would come to him—was he absolutely sure?

The last question led to more and more visits to Germany. There was something eerie, even unreal, about the whole thing. The strangest thing was the innkeeper himself. There he stood in the lobby, or in the dining room, keeping an eye on his employees and greeting the guests. He was the typical genial host in his Bavarian shorts. But now Casimir wondered whether that outfit was meant to suggest that Otto was not from Prussia, in order to make himself less identifiable. Or perhaps it was in memory of his Hitlerian hero who had made his initial bid for power in Munich and had loved his hideaway in Berchtesgaden. Still, the innkeeper had that kindly twinkle in his eye, that welcoming smile, that look of a kindly old uncle. But Casimir also saw the face of the savage who had ripped his family apart. As Casimir sat again and again in the dining hall, he knew something that no one else knew—the innkeeper and the savage were one and the same man.

Casimir was desperate to find a way to prove what he knew in his mind's eye. One day, he impulsively made a dire move as he sat in the dining room and the innkeeper came near his table. Casimir waited until Otto had passed the table and was walking toward the kitchen. Then he called out loudly and sharply:

"Mueller."

There was a pause. The heavy-set innkeeper stopped dead in his tracks. Slowly he looked back at Casimir, his face a frozen mask. Then he turned slowly and retraced his steps until he stood over Casimir's table:

"Did you call?" he said craftily.

Casimir could hardly speak, but hatred was stronger than fear, and it created the words:

"Yes," he said, "I was calling for Franz Mueller." He watched the face which had a slight twitch of one eyelid, but was otherwise impassive:

"I don't know anyone by that name," said the innkeeper deliberately, as his eyes searched the face of the sitting man without recognition. He could not place the man he had seen only as a boy, in a different place, in a different world.

Casimir was stymied once again. He went home where he began to lay his final plans. The frustration was so great that he began to entertain the extreme solution—he must kill the innkeeper even if it led to his own arrest and prosecution. He had to do it. No one else would. Nothing could save Otto Franz Mueller now, and nothing could save Casimir from throwing his own future to the wind.

The day came when Casimir packed his small suitcase in which he had made a hidden compartment for the gun. He knew how to get by customs because of the many times he had made the same trip—the customs inspectors had a pattern that could be avoided. At the inn, he had dinner as usual, but this time he stayed late until closing time. He was the last customer to walk out. Outside on the street, he waited until the heavy-set man closed up the inn and walked down the dark street toward his home. Casimir followed as his right hand felt for the metal object in his pocket. Bit by bit, he gained on the innkeeper until he was within ten feet, then five feet. It was time!

Casimir felt that the innkeeper knew that there was someone behind him, but he would not turn. Had he turned that face toward Casimir, he would have been dead. But when it came time for Casimir to pull the gun and shoot into the man's back, his hand stopped in midair. He walked on without doing it. And eventually he dropped back.

Casimir had not changed his mind—it was just that he could not degrade himself by just shooting another human being in the back on a dark night. In some way, despite everything, there was a remnant of pride in himself that would not let him do something that was so much like the savage himself. Casimir walked away.

At home in Poland, he reviewed it all again a hundred times. Again he decided that he had to do it for the sake of his parents, no matter what. But, just when Casimir had packed his suitcase once more with the gun and the shells in the secret compartment, there was an extraordinary event. As Casimir was about to leave, a stranger appeared on his doorstep. His visitor was a little man with a briefcase full of papers. It was the man from the war crimes organization. Casimir invited him in, and they sat in upholstered chairs facing each other.

"I've come to you," said the man, "because we have a lot of experience with the kind of thing you are dealing with, and I have some personal experience with the pain that you are in. I don't know what you may be planning now, but we have a lot of people who want to take matters into their own hands. I started to do that myself."

Saul Lapinski sat looking intensely at Casimir as if he could read his mind, and then he continued:

"I'm a Jew and you are Catholic, but at this moment, we are one person. I've learned to hate so much that I never do anything impulsive, and you must learn that too."

Casimir just sat, speechless. Lapinski wanted to finish his message:

"There's another thing you must learn. Move away from yourself and take the broad picture. There are thousands of Germans who participated in the death camps, and they have quietly disappeared into the post-war generation. There are Japanese citizens who were involved in the rape of Nanking where more people were murdered than in Hiroshima and Nagasaki combined. There are thousands of Khmer Rouge who took part in the massacres in Cambodia. There are thousands of Russians who took part in the looting, raping, and murder that Alexander Solzhenitsyn described in *Prussian Nights*. And there was the massacre of some ten thousand Polish officers at Ratyn. There are countless Serbs and Muslims who carry responsibility for the death of innocents. And each time there is a revolution in distant parts of the world, or a riot, there are sadistic people who come out of the woodwork. Do you know where most of these people are now?"

Casimir mumbled. Lapinski went on:

"They are mostly at home, doing regular jobs, and no more detectable to anyone else than your innkeeper. Listen to me carefully. We can do nothing to change all these human beings— there are always people who turn sadistic drives into action whenever they think they will never be found out. Everyone is not like that, thanks be to God, but there are thousands of humans who are. Crimes should never be forgotten, and we must seek for war criminals as long as we live, as long as they live, as long as we can breathe. But, to win, you must share my hatred enough to let one of our people handle your case, so that it does not fail. If you want to be active, join our group and work on other cases. So far, maybe you don't know how to turn your hate in the right direction."

Lapinski just sat. Casimir just sat. They spoke only a few more words, and Lapinski went home.

After this meeting, Casimir could not rest and could not sleep—he paced back and forth in his room at night. But a week later, a great calm came over him, and he pulled the shiny revolver out of its secret compartment. He moved it back and forth from one hand to the other. But finally, he stopped this strange exchange and walked slowly over to his bookcase where he placed the gun in back of the books. Then he walked over to the telephone and made a long distance call:

"Hello, is this Mr. Lapinski?" he asked.

"Yes," said the voice.

Casimir was very deliberate now, all his senses directed toward the distant voice:

"Tell me, Mr. Lapinski, are you sure you will never give up on my case?"

Lapinski answered dryly in one word:

"Never."

Casimir was breathing more easily and his muscles relaxed. He asked another question:

"Can you give me a different case to work on?"

It was such a simple question.

INTIMATE ILLUSION

She was cute and only nineteen, and he was fifteen years older. But Linda Colby was very much a woman and had very little patience for all the mockery and bravado of boys in her own age group. She looked straight into men's eyes, and she engaged them in spontaneous, easy-going conversation which quickly became personal. She was seductive in a very natural way. It was no surprise that Ronald Devereux was very much taken with her. He was not from town, but he had met her at a dance, and soon he was seeing her at every opportunity. It was all moving very fast, and they were obviously smitten.

Of course, their friends and relatives reacted with that traditional antipathy reserved for attachments between people whose ages don't match. There were those who hated to see an older man get a younger woman, and there were young women her age who hated to see Linda sporting about with the handsome and fully established Ronald Devereux. Only her parents' anxiety may have been fully genuine, and even they may not have worried about the right things.

The gossiping whispers about them were the usual:

"What's a man his age doing with a young girl like that? He'll enjoy her and then forget her."

Others focussed upon Linda:

"What does a girl that age know about love or what it means to the rest of her life?"

Relatives and friends all declared that she had the frail judgment of her age. But these interlopers into her heart had no idea what she felt or needed, so they just talked and talked. Linda countered with plaintive little assertions:

"It's the real thing," she said. "I just know it."

The attention that Ronald poured upon his new-found love was without limit. He reveled in the effect he had upon Linda's heart, and he spared no blandishments. The young boys who had admired Linda in the past had tried to gain her attention by daring feats and glib speech. But Ronald knew about gifts of flowers, chocolates, perfumes, and things to wear. All the attention pleased her, but there was more to it than that—they were both in love.

There was very little talk between them about the truth of their love—it was simply there. And in the end, it came down to that final love scene in which a man wants to possess a woman who wants to be possessed.

It came about one evening when they stopped in his apartment after dining out. She leaned toward him on the couch, and he kissed her and enveloped her in his arms as their excitement grew. It seemed as if nothing could hold them back now—and yet something did.

It was a peculiar interruption which should have been a minor event, and yet, like a shearing wind, it was able to twist events into a fresh direction. Until that instant, Linda had admired this man as an idol, an intimate illusion. But at this moment, the idol crashed as she saw his animal passions, and he suddenly became an earthy symbol. After all, it was her first time, and with his total transfiguration, she was overcome by an impulse to say what she felt. As they lay there on the couch, her mouth close to his ear, she whispered a fateful sentence:

"You're just like all the rest, after all," she murmured.

Ronald Devereux became very still, all his lovemaking suspended except for the way he was breathing hard. He wondered why he should have to defend his impulse and his actions, but he tried:

"I love you, Linda," he said.

"I know, I know," she responded, as she wrapped herself around him again.

But the full impact of her phrase had struck him hard because he wanted love and sex, not sex alone. Suddenly, he fully understood what had transpired between them in the months before. He understood that she had seen him as some great illusion, as everything that her girlish dreams could worship. She wanted that great illusion—and he was no illusion.

Ronald wasn't mad at her, but the spell was broken, and he pulled away.

Later Linda didn't know if she was glad or sorry. In one sense she was pleased because she could, once again, see him as different. It was very special of him, she thought, to let her sentence stop him in the heat of the moment. But it had never crossed her mind that her spontaneous remark could have lasting consequences, might even estrange them.

As the months went by, Linda tried to renew their close bonds. She hinted and then candidly told him that she really wanted an intimate relationship with him. But Ronald was deeply convinced that she loved only that great illusion of an idealized lover conjured up by her imagination—and it was all something well beyond what he could be, or even wanted to be. So their love hung there like a tattered flag that had seen grander days.

In her consternation, Linda did one smart thing. She thought about her friend Anna who was older and appeared to have been perfectly happy with the man she loved before marriage, and perfectly happy with him after eight years of married life. Anna must know something, must be doing something right. So Linda sought her out, and they sat in Anna's kitchen when everyone else was at work or school. She told Anna the whole story—even the intimate details. Then she asked the question:

"Did I do something wrong?"

Anna was amused:

"I certainly would not have said it," she responded.

"But Anna," persisted Linda, "it was an honest expression of how I felt at that very moment. Would you have me hide it? Is that any way to start out with a man you want to marry?"

Linda thought she had posed a difficult philosophical question about life and honesty. But Anna saw the answer right away:

"You said it too soon, and you said it at the wrong moment."

Linda was quite shocked that someone else saw the answer so easily—she even tried to present more reasons for having spoken at that moment, but none of the reasons were good enough.

In time, Linda and Ronald grew further and further apart, and one day he was transferred to a job in California while she stayed in New York. It led to less and less contact, and, in the end, even the letters stopped.

Linda's family was much relieved a few years later when she found a man her own age and married him. His name was Oliver and he was a perfectly presentable man, if not a knight in shining armor. All of Linda's friends were convinced that they had saved her from that older man. They had fixed everything—put all the parts of the puzzle back to where they should have been. They felt much better, as if somehow it was part of their business, and they had a common phrase to describe it:

"They came back to their senses."

Linda got along reasonably well with Oliver. She had no passion, but she had nice children—a daughter named Clara and a son they called Kip. But she often became moody, and Oliver suffered from that. He had no idea why she was like that.

Linda's thoughts often lingered upon her youthful illusion in which a man and woman could love without those animal passions. She was well beyond that now, and time had moved on. But when Linda was falling asleep or awakened in the middle of the night, her thoughts would wander back to that critical moment when she almost made love with Ronald. As in a familiar fairy tale, these thoughts would linger on until deep sleep finally rubbed them out. And when she actually dreamed in the night, it was often Ronald who was lying there next to her. The feeling that came with the dream would last for hours, even after she woke up.

Only Linda's lifelong vision of a perfect man had survived. She had kept the great illusion, the intimate illusion—the one she had preserved in a moment of candor.

Once in a while she met with Anna, and she admitted to her that she was plagued by a feeling that maybe she had missed her chance. She spoke of that intimate illusion she had conjured up about an ideal man, and she wondered if Ronald might have been the one.

Now there was nothing to do but live out her life as best she could. But for the next twenty years of her life, she lived with a deep hollow spot that she could never rub away—her only con-solation was the thought that life was like that for a lot of people.

Ronald had become all wrapped up in his new life in California and eventually met and married a woman his own age. Within two years, they were divorced. His bachelor life was all right, but it wasn't much. He had a few affairs, and not one of those women whispered in his ear. But none of these relation-ships meant much to him.

When Ronald thought about Linda, he convinced himself that it was all past history. But one day about twenty years later, he was sitting alone on a Saturday afternoon and started thinking about Linda again. And he remembered the awkward way in which he had preserved his integrity, but lost the woman. He became preoccupied by a single thought which soon haunted him—that Linda was still out there somewhere. He knew nothing about Linda's marriage, so he decided to write her a note:

> *Dear Linda,*
> *I think of you often and wonder how life is treating you. I'm coming East next month. Maybe we could have dinner.*
>
> > *Yours always,*
> > *Ronald*

Linda was dumbfounded! Until this moment her conflict had been subdued, if not settled. But now, with the coming of spring came this little note, and it disturbed her more than she wanted to believe. For twenty years she had lived with a suspicion that she had missed the great love of her life, and yet she could not put aside the fact that she was a married woman with children. The resignation with which Linda lived was suddenly threatened by this voice from the past. A stark question came to her mind, and she could not completely repress it: "Is this my second chance?"

Linda was by now a mature woman, so she quickly smothered that thought and wanted to be perfectly honest with her husband. She had never told Oliver about Ronald, and now she decided that she must say something. She chose to say that an old boyfriend would be in town, and she casually admitted her desire to see him—just to satisfy her curiosity about what he was like now. The explanation was true, but it was only half the truth, and that prompted her to try to set things completely right. So she asked Oliver if he would accompany her to this dinner with the old boyfriend. She supported the idea with another question: "Aren't you curious to see what he's like?" Oliver was not a bit curious about the boyfriend, but he wanted to be congenial as usual:

"We might do that if you like," he said. "When is he coming?"

"I think it's the first week of next month, on Tuesday, the twenty-fourth," Linda explained.

"I can't do that," said Oliver. "That's the week I have to close a contract in Chicago for the firm."

"Oh dear," murmured Linda, "I am really curious."

"Why don't you go ahead?" said her husband.

He left it like that and so did she. Oliver had very little passion within himself, so jealousy was not a part of his makeup.

Tuesday, the twenty-fourth, came around, and it was a day filled with excitement. Oliver had left for Chicago, so Linda paced back and forth all morning until the phone call came from Ronald who was already in town:

"I'm down at the Algonquin Hotel," he said. "Do you want to have dinner here or somewhere else?"

Linda was on the brink of telling him about her husband, but once again she held off.

"I don't mind where we meet," she said, but quickly added this:

"There's a good restaurant on Central Avenue; I'll tell you how to get there." Linda told the kids she was going out, and Clara became very curious:

"Out with an old boyfriend, eh? Does Dad know?"

"Of course he knows. It's just for curiosity." Linda was using that same phrase again.

At seven-thirty Linda was out the door. She was all dressed up and nervous. Her mind was racing with all those questions: "What was he like now?" "Would she get the old feeling about him?" "Was she wise to even be doing this?"

Clara watched her mother drive out—she felt a little unsettled. Good old Mom going out with an old boyfriend? It created a slightly threatening atmosphere for herself. Clara spent the evening watching television and calling friends. She ate more snacks than usual, and then she tried reading, but she soon went back to television and phone calls.

It was late when Linda came home, and Clara was at the door:

"How was it?" she asked.

"Oh, we had a good time, reminiscing and all that."

Clara wanted more than that, so she tried a few more questions. Her mother wouldn't say anything more about it.

After that, Linda's life with Oliver went on much the same. She was really home to stay, but there were some subtle changes. She was no longer moody, and Oliver was pleased. She felt other changes within herself, but never discussed them with the family. She was not thrilled about life, but it was better, and she was less preoccupied with the past. At night she slept better and had fewer dreams.

The only person she talked to about her meeting with Ronald was her friend Anna. She confided in her, at least partially, and Anna promised not to say anything. But Linda described only the dinner and Ronald's appearance and all the things he said. Anna, like Clara, wanted more about what kept Linda out so late, but that information never came. Linda did tell her one thing more:

"I'm not as bothered by my old obsession, by that intimate illusion I carried around with me about my first love."

That statement just tantalized Anna more:

"Is that because he didn't look as good?"

"No," said Linda, "he looked terrific."

"Well then," persisted Anna, "is it because..."

She stopped in mid-sentence. She had almost gone too far. And yet she desperately wanted to know what happened on that mysterious night. Did Linda fling herself daringly forward, or did she just become more realistic, or did she finally see him as an old man? Anna hoped her friend would open up and tell her all the mysteries of that special night. But that never happened. All the events of that single night were shrouded under those banks of memories in which Linda lived.

Anna could only watch her friend carefully, and she certainly did that. She studied her face for any little sign—all without success. But one thing was becoming perfectly clear. Linda was different! That air of distraction was gone, and she obviously knew something or understood something. She was no longer bothered by that obsession, that sense of missing out on life, that marvelous, but maddening, intimate illusion.

INHERIT THE EARTH

"Endicott is not assertive enough. He's so mild-mannered, so meek, that he will never amount to anything."

Roger Talbot's old refrain to his wife Lillian reflected their dissatisfaction with their only son who never accepted their way of life. Roger was a broker with a respectable education in business administration and later training in an investment house, so he understood the vagaries of the market. But in the course of his training, he had never taken a single course in philosophy, religion, science, psychology, or literature. The other brokers who worked with Roger in the investment house had the same narrow education, so they considered him an unqualified success with all the knowledge he needed. The trouble was that his son Endicott was totally preoccupied with literature, religion, and philosophy, so they could not communicate.

Roger was fully satisfied with himself, and he suffered no introspection because he and his peers in the investment business measured everything by the position achieved on those lengthy charts and tables produced by the brokerage firm. Happiness simply rose and fell with the market.

Of course, like all his cohorts, Roger professed the need for

117

other values in life, and he would often say, "There is more to life than money." But this was just talk. Watching his life pattern, it was clear that such phrases were only part of the language he had learned to use—it had nothing to do with anything he understood or practiced. In fact, the absence of any personal philosophy was a great protective curtain that shielded Roger from moral doubts and centered his only concerns upon the reliability of his work with investments.

Roger's wife Lillian fit in well with his standards, and she manifested it amply on their twenty-fifth wedding anniversary:

"I was thinking back upon our life," she said. "We live in a fine neighborhood, we have everything we want, and we have traveled extensively, just as we imagined we would when we first met."

"I'm pleased to hear you say it," Roger rejoined.

He was glad to know that his wife was happy, but he was even more pleased that she seemed to recognize that all these good things were the result of his signal success in the market. He continued:

"My financial philosophy has created our success. I invested only after careful study of every prospectus, always in search of firms with convincing growth capacity—I kept my eye on long-term gains and never gambled upon hot tips for quick gains. When you invest wisely, it is rarely necessary to panic when the market is unstable."

Roger licked his lips as he spoke. Lillian had heard his investment philosophy many, many times, but she never doubted its wisdom since the evidence of its success surrounded her. She always responded to his repetition of this simple idea by acting as if it were a recent and great discovery of his own. That was one of the prime reasons for the success of their marriage.

The Talbots appeared to be impervious to calamity, but it was galling to Roger that there was a weak spot that he could never incorporate into his management portfolio. The weak spot was the next generation—that natural product of union by marriage which is the least manageable and which displaces more space with every year that passes.

The Talbots' only son Endicott had started out all right in elementary school and in high school. Like his father, the boy was fitting into society without disturbing the waters, and he achieved the proper grades and the recognition expected of a broker's son. But then he went to college at an ivy league school. The Talbots should have foreseen an upcoming upheaval the first day that Endicott registered for college. He signed up for courses in philosophy, literature, religion, and psychology. Obviously these choices were not what Roger would have selected for his son, but he accepted them as a manifestation of class. He assumed that this was only a phase of college life, to be followed by courses in useful subjects such as business administration or science. Never in a thousand years would it have occurred to Roger Talbot that the courses selected by his son could have any effect upon the practical aspects of life. He thought that this kind of education was meant to be practiced as a kind of hobby, as a pastime unrelated to the actual decisions of daily living and career. It never crossed his mind that anyone might want to live according to the thoughts expressed by ancient sages.

Roger was quite surprised at Thanksgiving vacation when Endicott asked him to sit down and discuss their family philosophy of life. Roger still did not suspect any turmoil. For him, a philosophy of life had to do with a series of practical decisions about such things as how one planned to earn a living, how and where one expected to live, and with whom one might expect to associate.

The father and son discussion began amiably:

"Why don't you start the ball rolling," said Roger paternally.

That was his first mistake. Endicott accepted:

"I always start out with Aristotle," said Endicott. "He produced much of the world's great philosophy and had a direct bearing upon many of our ideas today. After Aristotle, I think of Sophocles and Euripides, and then Homer and Virgil, and of course, Cicero. Their writing has taught me to examine myself and the meaning of life—to search for meaning in the self."

Roger was baffled, his composure already on edge. It wasn't so much that there was any disagreement, but rather that there couldn't be any disagreement since Roger had never read anything written by any of these men. He could have simply admitted his ignorance, but that would have weakened his paternal role, so Roger tried to bypass the situation:

"Well," he said, you certainly named the great philosophers, but I have tried to formulate my own life philosophy on more practical, more modern terms."

"That is certainly legitimate," said Endicott, "and that is the very next step that I usually follow. Among the more modern thinkers, I think of Turgenev, Tolstoy, Balzac, and the American writers like Thoreau, Melville, Emerson, Hawthorne, and Henry James."

Things had taken another bad turn, but Roger glimpsed a rescuing possibility. For some reason that he could not remember, he had read *Moby Dick* during a lull in one of his vacations. Here was his chance!

"*Moby Dick* was a great adventure story," he exclaimed. "I read the book from cover to cover, and it gave me a better understanding of the life of whales which has certainly been the subject of many television programs. Melville knew what he was talking about because he had been at sea."

Endicott looked puzzled:

"Sure Dad," he said, "but you know, of course, that *Moby Dick* was not really about whales. I mean, the white whale was certainly a part of it, but the real meaning of the story was about people, not whales."

Roger was baffled again and didn't know how to proceed from there. The conversation did not develop well—and since there had been no significant meaning from the start, one would have to admit that the discussion on philosophy had never amounted to anything. But Endicott made one last desperate try:

"I think the most important thing we do in life is to generate a passion about what we stand for and then to actually mold our lives according to our philosophy."

Roger nodded his head because he thought he could respond to that one:

"Well, yes," he said, "I formed an early concept of myself as a broker. I knew what I wanted to be. The trouble with you is that you're not aggressive enough about your life—you need to go after a career, after a position that will give you an adequate income and some personal standing. You're too meek. Yes, that's it. You're too meek about everything. You need to assert yourself in some area that leads to an executive position."

Endicott thought he could make him understand:

"I certainly agree that a person has to find a place in life. But I don't care a bit about empowerment of either men or women. I don't want to just earn a lot of money or become an administrator running the lives of other people. A person should commit himself or herself to producing something original, or a person should be devoted to the service of others. That's the way I want to define myself."

"Well," said his father, "that's right, but it's all part of the same thing, isn't it?"

Endicott looked blankly at his father. He wasn't angry at him, but he could see that they didn't talk the same language. It was as close as Roger and his son ever came to an adult father-son exchange, and since it failed, it was never repeated.

Endicott tried talking with his mother, and she was sympathetic. Lillian and Endicott had a nice chat, but it was soon apparent to Endicott that his mother's values were the same as his father's. It led nowhere. Endicott made one more urgent try with his mother. He brought up the subject of "self" again, of the meaning of being something inside, of having a purpose in life other than power and money. His mother responded in her kind and bland manner with a truism:

"Yes," she said, "we should all be ourselves and not try to be something we are not, but you do need to get established in life. You're so meek about everything, as your father always says, that the world will not recognize you as an established person unless you achieve some kind of status."

Endicott knew then that she didn't have the slightest idea what he was talking about. It made him feel lonely, as if he were out in the middle of the world on his own. He turned away from his parents and back to his professors. He chose Professor Billingham because he was young, well outside of his parents' generation, and always accessible. He made Endicott feel as if he were involved in world events:

"Good literature," said the professor, "can deal with characters that are true to life, or it can concern itself with imagination. In the second instance, however, there is still some kind of tie to reality because the author who invents these characters is himself a part of this world and cannot create out of a vacuum—part of his life experience comes through."

Endicott could plunge into a discussion like this. Here was reality generated by literature and history, by an informed view of the universe, and by the intellectual growth of people over the centuries. Endicott felt less lonely than with his father and mother, and he talked with the professor for an hour and a half until Professor Billingham had to go to a class.

For many weeks, Endicott and Professor Billingham renewed their discussions. Endicott believed that he was finally engrossed in the real world, and Professor Billingham was deeply satisfied that his professorial intellect was used to improve a young mind. But as the meetings continued, Endicott became disillusioned. It started one day as he watched the professor holding forth. It wasn't so much what the professor was saying as it was that

Endicott began to look at the professor himself.

Professor Billingham sat behind his big desk. Every so often he would rotate in his swivel chair toward the window where he seemed to derive his ideas from the atmosphere beyond the room. There was a certain detachment from everything around him as he recalled the great references from literature and history. Endicott began to speculate upon what the professor must have been like as a student—probably a pest. Endicott could see him in high school, far-removed from the rest of the students and without any of the social standing that he now enjoyed. No doubt he annoyed most of the other students since he was probably not interested in sports, entertainment, adventure, or social events.

Endicott noticed that the professor's fingernails were bitten and short, that his suit was rumpled, and that he never shined his shoes. He usually wore a white shirt, but when he selected one with color or stripes, it never matched the rest of his clothes. Endicott watched him as he swung back toward his desk surveying the room and his audience of one. This was really the professor's base of operation—this and the podium where he gave his lectures.

Endicott noticed another thing about the professor. Whenever there was a faculty senate meeting, or a meeting with the Dean, the professor would drop all his philosophy and become totally preoccupied with the power struggles of his department in the university. Endicott began to wonder what the professor would be like if someone took away his desk, his swivel chair, and his office. That caused an uncomfortable image to appear. The professor, thrown suddenly into the surrounding world and forced to undertake some other job, might not look like much at all.

Endicott came a few more times for these intellectual exercises, and then he reached a decision. He went back to his father and mother and dropped the bombshell!

"I've decided to drop out of college," he said.

Roger and Lillian went through the usual shock. They didn't really care about education and learning, but they viewed college as a stepping stone. They bombarded their son with warnings, but this time Endicott was remarkably determined—it had never occurred to Roger that the assertiveness that he had been requesting could be turned against himself. So Roger tried to find a new approach to his son by directing the argument toward something he considered more practical, while pretending to agree with his son:

"I respect your position," he said. "Perhaps we can get you started in the business."

Endicott knew immediately that "the business" could mean only one thing—the investment house. He responded fast and with a cutting tone in his voice:

"That's the last thing I want to do."

Roger and Lillian were crestfallen, and Roger now felt he had reason to be annoyed. He raised his voice:

"O.K.," he said. "You tell us what you're going to do."

Much to his surprise, Endicott had an immediate answer.

"I'm going to South America. There's a mission down there which serves the needs of orphans and children whose parents are desperately poor. I'm going to work for them. The mission has already accepted me, if you will sign the papers."

Now Roger felt that he was entitled to be indignant:

"What in the world do you think this is going to do for you? What's it going to lead to?"

Endicott responded calmly, but without backing off:

"Why does it have to lead to anything else? It's a goal in itself."

"But when you come back, what will you do?" Roger and Lillian said, almost in unison.

"Maybe I won't come back. I may just make that my whole life."

The parental shock was devastating. After that moment, the discussion was fruitless, and many weeks of agony followed as Roger tried to find out what kind of mission service, or cult, had captured his son. It turned out to be a perfectly respectable church mission, although perhaps a little remote from the main-line churches.

Eventually Endicott got his way, not by anger or demands, but by maintaining an attitude of extraordinary determination. His mind, his attitude, even his posture, were fixed in one direction. Eventually there was a final departure for South America and a sad farewell at the airport.

The next eight years had a sense of unreality for the Talbots. All their plans for their son had vanished overnight. They couldn't understand how it could all have happened so fast. Endicott was never hostile to his parents, and he wrote letters every few weeks. He returned home for holidays, and each time, the Talbots thought he might announce that he was coming home for good. But he never did.

On the eighth year, disaster struck! A phone call came through from someone at the mission. The caller was very sorry to announce that Endicott had contracted a serious form of malaria. Complications had set in, and Endicott was in critical condition. The Talbots came to life. They rushed to make reservations for a plane to South America. But, by the time they had their reservations and their bags packed, a second phone call came through with the terrible news. Endicott was dead!

It was unbelievable. The extended Talbot family gathered. Arrangements were made for the body to be shipped home. All was sorrow and hopelessness. Friends and neighbors felt very sorry for the Talbots, not just because of Endicott's death, but because they knew that Endicott had never followed in his father's footsteps, had never amounted to very much. They regarded Endicott as a wastrel. They were like people who had come to witness a disaster—it excited them, left them thankful that it had not happened in their family, and required only that they put on their most sympathetic faces.

The Talbots' family minister spoke first at the funeral service, and he began by saying all the right things, so the assembled guests listened approvingly. Then he made a mistake—he asked whether there was anyone else who wanted to speak. At first no one moved, but some of them looked around, and they did notice a stranger in their midst. He was seated near the back of the church looking expectant—as if he thought that there was much more to say. When the stranger saw that no one else would volunteer, he rose to his feet and walked slowly, but deliberately, toward the front of the church. He walked up the steps leading to the pulpit and took his place at the center of it. He began to address them with a strong Hispanic pattern of speech, but there was no mistaking his powerful message. He started casually:

"I am the director of a mission house in South America, and I have come to express my grief to Endicott's parents and friends and to share the richness of his life."

The congregation did not privately acknowledge the richness of Endicott's life. They expected words of praise which would hint at the wasted life to be recovered in the kingdom of heaven. There was an entrenched satisfaction in that expectation. That was the way things were supposed to be said. The stranger continued in a different vein:

"Eight years ago a young man came to our organization who wanted only one thing; he wanted a chance to work with the children. He said he didn't care about salary or position as long as he had shelter and food, so I was able to take him on immediately. I thought Endicott was a dreamer, a visionary, but I never thought he would stick with it. As time passed I watched with amazement at the determination on his face—the determination to simply do the work. He never talked about status, empowerment, self-assertion, or public relations—he never thought any of these things were important.

The assembled guests were now becoming restless. The stranger seemed to be downgrading all the words which they breathed in and breathed out every day. The visitor resumed:

"Endicott just worked every day for the children, as if it were his last day. It has been a great lesson for me."

The whole service was taking an unexpected turn, and the guests were ill at ease. Still the stranger continued:

"I want to thank Endicott's parents and all of you who, by your example, taught him to dedicate himself to the service of other people."

There were a few murmurs among the assembled guests, and they shuffled their feet. The stranger was very deliberate now:

"Some people said that Endicott was too meek, but I tell you that Endicott was the closest thing to a saint that I have ever known."

The eulogy was over, but the man remained standing in stony silence. He looked searchingly from one face to another, as if he were about to question each one separately. There was a stifling tension permeating the quiet of the church, as if he were about to accuse the guests directly. But instead he bowed his head, stood silently in prayer, and then slowly walked down the stairs, down the aisle, and out of the church.

After the service, everyone gathered outside to see the stranger, but he had vanished—he had said his piece.

What of all the guests? They continued to mill around aimlessly, pursued by the words of a stranger. They were in an agitated state. Several were overheard complaining that the stranger's remarks were not appropriate to a funeral service. Whenever they came face to face with the Talbots, they recovered their facial expressions of sympathy and commiseration. The Talbots themselves were not sure what had happened.

WHALE SONGS AND THE WAKE AT SEA

John Schneider was happiest when he was at sea. He had always worked there, harvesting the food from the sea. Every day was different out there, and for a man who knew how to read the sea, there was never a time when he wanted to escape from it.

Before he turned to whales for a living, John Schneider had earned money by running a small fishing operation with two crew members to help pull in the nets. Just after the first World War, he had saved enough money to buy a seventy-foot vessel that could be used to hunt for whales. It was an old ship, and it was not a very modern operation. But the crew used that deadly weapon invented in Norway to pack an explosive head in the harpoon to kill the whales more rapidly. The equipment also allowed air to be pumped into the whale and keep it afloat, so that they could harvest whales that were as long as the boat.

The pattern was always the same. The ship moved slowly over the feeding ground of the whales where the sea was relatively shallow—only a hundred feet or so. The ship cruised along, rolling and pitching as the waves lifted it and let it down again and again. When Schneider and his men had located the right place, whales were all around them—mostly hump-backed whales, fin whales, minke whales, pilot whales, and a few right whales. Each kind of whale had a distinctive spout, so John could identify them from afar. When the whales were very close, John watched until he had fixed upon the one he wanted. Then he readied his men. As the great beast rose again, they fired the shot and the deadly load pierced the side of the whale. Blood appeared on the surface of the water, and it increased amidst the churning foam where the whale made a last struggle for life. Even with the explosion, it could take an hour for death to come. In the end, there was only blood, and later, parts of the whale that littered the surface of the water. The ship cruised upon a huge pool of blood.

For John and his men, it was a way of life. They took from the sea, and then they took again, and again.

But there was a great irony in John Schneider's life. It had taken him so many years to save enough money to own his own ship, old as it was, that by the time he had his own operation, the great whaling days were drawing to a close. Most American whaling ships had sailed their last voyages, and after World War II, the International Whaling Convention was signed in Washington. Whale hunting was much restricted, but the regulations were not consistently enforced, so John's relatively small operation continued to hunt the whales that were not as tightly controlled. Eventually the moratorium on whaling did cut back on John's business. He became so mad and so desperate that he gave up his own ship and, mournfully, signed up to work for a Norwegian company that disregarded the whaling limits. That took him away from his American coastline where he had cruised the New England coast and far beyond it, both north and south. Working for the Norwegians wasn't like working in his own waters for himself, but it was a living. When he felt he had enough money to retire, he pulled out of it and came back home to New England.

But John Schneider could not keep off the water. He loved the sea so much that he bought a small wooden sailboat to cruise the waters, without all the fishing gear and without any purpose, except to enjoy the sea. Yes, he was one of those men who loved to sail alone. He would have liked to sail across the ocean, but he had neither the boat for it, nor the energy. But he could go out all day with sails unfurled. On those days, all alone, John would cruise out to sea for twenty or thirty miles. There he felt at one with the universe, never tiring of the swells, the sea smell, the wind, and the sounds of the water.

When John sailed alone, he would at times come upon the very herds of whales that he had hunted. After all, those that got away could live into their sixties too, just like him. And a few might live to be eighty years old, just about when he would get that old. They came back into the same waters where they were born and where they hunted, into the same waters where John had hunted them. As long as John had lived by killing whales, he had seen them as something that nature provided for man to harvest. But now, more and more, John watched them as they raised their young, as they played together, or shot out of the water in what seemed like sheer pleasure. More and more, he loved the whales. He left them alone, and they left him alone. Rising next to his sailboat, they were often more than twice the size of his boat, but he knew that they were not dangerous to him.

People who didn't know whales would never have believed that these leviathans might recognize John Schneider; but John knew how smart they were, and he believed that they knew him. So bit by bit, this man, who lived on the sea and by the sea, felt more and more at one with the whales amongst which he sailed.

John always knew how to expect their next appearance. Those telltale bubbles appeared as the whales formed curtains of air with which they rounded up the sea life that they would catch. There were also those clear circles of smooth water that appeared on the surface when the whales' powerful flukes swept the water below. And finally, the water turned green as the whales exchanged water below the surface. Of course, there was another way to know when they would be coming up. Whales liked to come up for air every ten minutes, so after a dive, John could look at his watch and know when the next appearance would be. A whale could hold its breath much longer than that, but most of them stuck to the ten or fifteen minute pattern.

Was there ever a beast like this that did not run away when its arch predator came amongst their huddled groups? Millions of years had taught the whales that there was no predator as big as they were, so they had not altered their pattern when they were attacked by harpoons and explosives. Slowly rising for air, they would play upon the surface, occasionally lifting a fluke into the air, or rising headfirst toward the sky and pausing to look at John and his boat. Then, once again, they would dive into the depths of the sea, raising their huge tails in order to gain the downward motion for the dive.

These were magic moments. Whenever John saw the telltale signs, he knew that his friends were about to appear. They were idyllic moments when John was most at one with the sea and the whales. Occasionally they would rest next to his boat, and he would reach toward their heads. And yet it was then that strange emotions arose, forming dangerous ties that reached from the sea toward the body of John Schneider. Yes, it was at these moments that he drifted into dreamy states in which his mind merged with the sea and the whales. Eyes half-closed, he watched those great tails, different for every whale, and he recognized each one as an individual. This led to his naming them, and soon there was George, Stella, Ida, Norman, Willy, Albert, and others. John began to relate to them as other living people, and he whispered the names of the older ones in reverence as he remembered how they had survived in the sea like him through those changing times. In this dreamy state of mind came the trouble. That was the great irony, that what John Schneider loved the most was what did him in.

As good a seaman as John would never have been caught in a storm that he couldn't handle. But one day he was dreaming too long amongst the whales, and he didn't watch the instruments or the horizon well enough. He talked to the whales until he fell asleep, and then he dreamed about them still. And by the time he woke up, the storm was upon him, and the fury of the wind and the water churned all around him.

If ever there was a sailor who could handle a storm it was John. He used everything he had learned to keep his boat from being knocked down, letting those great sails hit the water. He furled the sails as much as he could and kept only a weather helm. He made his boat strike the waves at an angle, and he never broached. But the terrible storm was too much, and the stays began to tear loose, and the weather helm began to rip. The surging waters were sweeping over the side and down the deck. John was really in danger now! He had come out upon the sea as he always had when he was young, but his strength was not as great as it used to be. And for a sailor who should have known better, John was not tethered to his boat. Those wonderful whales had kept his mind dreaming when it should have been at work. And when a great wave swept over the boat again, it caught the old man and lifted him from the deck.

The storm was over almost as quickly as it had come. But John was now floating in the water, and his sailboat was nowhere to be seen. All around him was the sea—no land, no boats, no people to call. John searched for some fragment from the boat, something he could hang on to. But he found nothing. He was all alone, really alone, as far as the eye could see.

But then he became aware of those familiar signs on the surface of the water—the bubbles, the green water, and the smooth patches. The whales appeared all around him. A glimmer of hope surfaced in John's heart—they were his friends, the ones he had known so long. Some of them had been in his sights, off and on, for over fifty years. They too, were getting old. But there were young ones too that he had met just last year. John's hope for life surged, just like the giants that came curiously around him. They knew John, but they had never seen him afloat like this.

For hours John continued to fight for his life. He swam on his back, or he treaded water. As his muscles gave out, he inhaled and held his breath so as to allow himself to submerge without struggle, until he had to come up again to take another breath. He was, in a sense, doing like the whales, submerging and rising again at intervals, only he had to come up every few minutes. At one point, a whale came up right beside him, and John's weary brain thought for a moment that he could be supported by it, or that he could grab hold of a fluke. But none of this was really possible. Still, John's last hope, the thing that kept him fighting so long, was the whales. They stayed all around him, so he was never alone.

But what were the whales thinking all this time? What were they to make of this unusual sight? Their former predator was dying amidst their feeding ground while they continued the patterns that had worked so well for them before the man. They made the rings of bubbles by which they rounded up their food. Then they gulped those thousands of gallons of water and fish until they closed their mouths and, with their tongues, pushed the water back out through the baleens to sift out the living things they ate. And they continued to play as they rolled over and lifted their flukes into the air. John Schneider recognized one of his old whales—it was the one he called George. At one point, George came up, lifted his head above water, and remained motionless, as he curiously examined the floating body of the man. Eventually, George slowly submerged again, and once more he started his fishing patterns and the playful motions that he shared with the rest of the pod.

The whales were all around John Schneider with their calls to each other. First there were the clicking sounds, as if they were trying to locate him more accurately in their midst. Then there were whistling sounds and the haunting cries. More and more of the great whales were gathering and calling to each other in this wake at sea.

Within the center of this great gathering of whales at sea was the desperately struggling body of John Schneider. During his great whaling days, he had been among them doing what he had learned to do, and now the whales still moved about with their ancient patterns. Did they recall his murderous harpoons, or did they remember the later friendly days when he reached for them at the side of his small boat? What passed through their minds lay there like a large question floating on the surface of the water. They made no effort to keep John afloat, but neither did they hate him nor harm him because they simply did not have the heart for it. So they rose and dived and rose again, and the last sound that John Schneider heard was the songs that came and went, and came again.

Born of American parents abroad, Philip Edward Duffy lived in France, Poland, Czechoslovakia, and America. A graduate of Columbia College and Medical School, he interned at the Long Island Division of Kings County Hospital and served a residency at the Hospital of the University of Pennsylvania.

As an Army reservist he was recalled to active service in the Far East, where he served as a medical officer during the Korean conflict. Subsequently he became Professor of Neurology at the State University of New York in Syracuse, and later Professor of Neuropathology and Director of the Neuropathology Division at the Columbia University College of Physicians and Surgeons. He is the author of many medical and scientific articles and a book on the astrocyte cells of the human brain. In addition, he was the editor and a contributor to a text and taped lecture series in neuropathology. Winner of the Joseph Mather Smith Prize, Philip Duffy also served for many years as a member of the editorial board of the *Journal of Neuropathology and Experimental Neurology.* He later became Professor Emeritus of Columbia University.

From his early life in Europe and America, through his medical career, and his varied experiences in military service in the Far East, Philip Duffy has remained an interested and perceptive observer of human nature. He expresses his observations in the fictional characters of his short stories. His first book of fiction, *Moments, A Collection of Short Stories,* was published in 1990 by

Chase Publishing. A second collection, *Undertones*, followed in 1996. These insightful and entertaining stories touch upon the life experience of all readers because they describe special moments that unexpectedly and radically alter people's lives.

In his newest collection of short stories, *The Head of the Bull*, Philip Duffy continues his explorations into the complexities of human experience with penetrating observations and often surprising results.

In addition to his writing activities, Philip Duffy is the past editor of the literary magazine, *Expressions*, and currently serves as a director of *My Country*, a magazine dedicated to American history. He and his wife Natalie make their home in western Connecticut.

Order Information

To order additional copies of *The Head of the Bull* or Philip Duffy's earlier collections of short stories, *Undertones* and *Moments*, check with your local book store, or contact:

Chase Publishing
P.O. Box 1200
Glen, NH 03838
Tel: 603-383-4166 Fax: 603-383-8162
http://www.chasepublishing.com

The Head of the Bull..................$12.95 plus $3.00 ea. shipping
(ISBN 0-9629651-3-8)

Undertones ....$10.95 plus $3.00 ea. shipping
(ISBN 0-9629651-1-1)

Moments....................................$9.95 plus $3.00 ea. shipping
(ISBN 0-9629651-0-3)

Please make checks payable to Chase Publishing